THEIR GUILTY PLEASURES

1940s. War alters lives, and for three women from different walks of life, the choices they make will change everything forever... Jenny Proctor is a well-to-do housewife with a demanding husband. She devotes her life to serving him – but when he enlists, she finds her voice ... and a new friendship with a young GI. Vibrant Rusty Dobbs is a prostitute by choice, making money from servicemen. But when she falls in love with an American captain, she hides her profession from him hoping that he will never find out... And finally, there is Sarah, a teenager who is drawn to Gunter, a prisoner of war – the enemy.

For my elder daughter Beverley, who survived a horrendous car crash with such bravery and courage. Whose mental attitude in the months that followed was incredible, and who never lost her sense of humour.

Amazing!

THEIR GUILTY PLEASURES

by

June Tate

Magna Large Print Books
Long Preston, North Yorkshire,
BD23 4ND, England.

British Library Cataloguing in Publication Data.

Tate, June
    Their guilty pleasures.

    A catalogue record of this book is
    available from the British Library

    ISBN   978-0-7505-3676-9

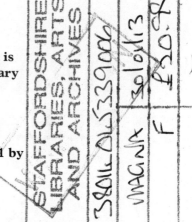

First published in Great Britain in 2011 by
Severn House Publishers Ltd.

Copyright © 2011 by June Tate

Cover illustration © Patricia Turner by arrangement with
Arcangel Images

The moral right of the author has been asserted

Published in Large Print 2013 by arrangement with
Severn House Publishers Ltd.

Magna Large Print is an imprint of Library Magna Books Ltd.

Printed and bound in Great Britain by
T.J. (International) Ltd., Cornwall, PL28 8RW

Acknowledgements

To Janet and Richard Cartwright in Stafford, who proved their friendship far beyond the call of duty. Ronnie, Beverley and I could not have managed without you. My grateful thanks.

Prologue

Jenny Procter stood at the French windows of her drawing room, looking out over the large garden before her. The rhododendron bushes were in full bloom, the horse chestnut trees full of leaf, and there was the promise of a bumper crop of fruit. Beyond one of the large lawns, the gardener was digging the earth and planting vegetables which had been started in the greenhouse. It was a peaceful scene, yet in Europe the Germans had swept through France. The phoney war was over and the nation stood ready to defend its coastline.

Adam Procter was to leave his prestigious post as bank manager at the National Provincial Bank and join the Hampshire Regiment. As an officer in the Territorial Army, it was to be expected, and Jenny stood wondering just how it would feel when his presence was no longer part of her daily life.

Her husband of fifteen years was heavy maintenance. Extremely fastidious about his appearance, demanding perfection in the ironing of his clothes, the upkeep of the home and the constant entertaining of his most wealthy clients, which with wartime rationing, was a headache for any housewife.

9

Jenny let out a deep sigh. She was tired. She had spent the previous days laundering, packing underwear and shirts – which, of course, had been meticulously ironed – and, in the odd moment, she felt it would be a relief when Adam was gone ... and immediately was overcome with a sense of guilt. After all, he would be transferred to France to fight the enemy. She gave a wry smile. It would have to be a brave man that had to face her husband. She knew that the staff at the bank tried their best to please their boss, rather than face his wrath. His quick temper would be another thing that she wouldn't miss either, concluded the lovely Mrs Procter as she made her way to the kitchen.

Adam Procter was in his office at the end of the day's banking, sipping a gin and tonic, bidding farewell to some of the senior members of the staff, introducing them to the man who would take his place. He had mixed emotions as he chatted, making polite conversation, anxious to get away, now the time had come. He had enjoyed his prestigious position in the bank and his standing in the upper echelon of society in the town and knew he would miss it, but he felt the rank of captain would offer some sort of compensation. He eventually took his leave, calling a taxi to take him home.

As the vehicle made its way along the Avenue towards Chilworth, he gave a soft smile of satisfaction. He had done well, achieved much in his life. Had reached a good position in business, had been able to afford a large house in a high-class neighbourhood and was married to a woman who was not only beautiful, but who also had been able to grow with him as he climbed the ladder of success. Yes, he had really made it, and when the war was over he would return to the bank and take his place in society once more. After all, the war couldn't last that long. It would be, in many ways, an adventure.

As a natural-born leader, he mused, he had enjoyed the military side and had thrived on the training – being in command. In one way, he was looking forward to the change. He liked a challenge, indeed he thrived on it!

Jenny heard the front door open. 'Is that you, darling?' she called.

Adam walked into the drawing room and taking off his jacket hung it carefully round the back of a chair. He loosened his tie as he walked towards his wife and gave her a brief kiss.

'How did today go?' she asked.

Adam walked over to the sideboard and poured two drinks. 'It was fine. Everyone was very kind; you know, lots of good wishes, lots of hand shaking, a few drinks. The new man seemed all right, but a bit weak I thought. Too nice by far! You need to have a firm grip at the top to keep your staff in control. But of course he's older – that, and the fact that he has bad eyesight, has kept him out of the forces.'

Jenny secretly thought how the staff would appreciate a man who wasn't so controlling and, irritated by Adam's attitude, said: 'Of course, he's had more years in banking than you. With so

11

much experience, he must know what he's doing, otherwise the bank wouldn't have kept him on.'

'Who knows!' With that Adam changed the subject. 'Is everything ready for tomorrow?'

'Yes, everything is packed, uniform pressed, shoes cleaned. All you have to do is pack your toiletries just before you go. I can't believe we have only twenty-four hours left and then you'll be on your way.'

He heard the note of uncertainty in her voice and saw the look of concern in her eyes. It suddenly hit him as to how much he was leaving behind. Until this moment there had been so much to do at the bank to prepare for the hand-over that he'd had little time to think. Suddenly, the reality of it all was painfully apparent.

He took Jenny into his arms and kissed her, wanting to feel the closeness of her, the comfort of her warm body. His kiss became more insistent as he felt her respond. He took her by the hand and led her upstairs to the bedroom.

Once there, he undressed her slowly, caressing her, kissing her, telling her how much he would miss her, until the two of them lay on the bed, their bodies entwined.

As Adam thrust himself inside her, Jenny sensed the desperation in his love-making. Unexpectedly, her husband had shown a certain vulnerability – but only for a moment. Knowing him as she did, she knew that he would soon be in control of his emotions once again. She opened her eyes and saw the relief on his face as, above her, he reached his climax. Yes, things were back to normal.

The following afternoon, a military car arrived at the house to take Adam, immaculately dressed in his uniform, to join his regiment; he handed his baggage to the driver and turned towards his wife.

'I'll call you when I know what's happening of course, but I'll be busy for the next couple of days, so don't worry if you don't hear from me. Take care.' He leaned forward and kissed her goodbye. There was no warmth or affection in his lips. It was a duty performed; his mind was now elsewhere.

Jenny watched the car drive away. She felt as if a weight had been lifted from her shoulders, and with a sense of relief, she walked back into the house. She was determined to fill her time and do something useful with her new-found freedom, but at the same time she was mindful of the dangers that lay ahead for her husband and prayed he would be safe.

One

It was almost three years to the day since Adam had left to join the army, Jenny mused as she opened a letter from him. So much had happened during the intervening years. Southampton had been decimated by the Blitz in 1940, and since then the war had escalated in Europe. Many children had been evacuated to other parts of the country, and a few were even taken abroad – some to the United States of America, others to Canada. This summer, the town had been invaded by American troops who would be using the docks to receive and send supplies – and their troops to the battlefields. Jenny was now on a committee set up to help them integrate into the British way of life, during their stay.

She read the letter. It was brief and to the point. Aware that censorship was essential, Adam, unable to say where he was, kept the details succinct. He was fine, the regiment was doing well, there had been some fighting, but he was unscathed. He hoped she was in good health, and he was happy that she was doing her bit for the war effort. There were no words of love or affection, except at the end he told her that he missed her. But it seemed a perfunctory remark – without meaning.

With a sigh, Jenny put the letter in a drawer

15

with the others. She'd answer it tonight, but now she was off to a meeting where she was to liaise with an officer in charge of the welfare of the American troops that had been arriving by the truckload. It had been decided to hold a dance at the Guildhall, to introduce the troops to the locals. Jenny herself was not at all sure this was a good idea, but realized that sooner or later the local dances would be full of the visiting troops anyway. She foresaw a certain amount of friction between the British boys – both the troops and the local boys who were yet to be called up – and the gregarious Yanks, with their superior uniforms and pockets full of money. The red-light district was doing a roaring trade, according to the police, which put even more pressure on them as they dealt with drunken brawls to try and keep the peace and *entente cordial* with the Americans.

Jenny made her way to the headquarters of the 14th Port and was taken to the office of Captain Brad Jackson. The soldier accompanying her tapped on the door and, being told to enter, announced her.

'Mrs Procter, sir.'

A tall man, with mid-brown hair and blue eyes, stood up and offered her his hand. 'Mrs Procter, how nice to meet you. Please sit down.'

His voice had a soft accent and was cultured, she noticed, not as loud and brash as some she'd heard on the High Street as the troops investigated their new surroundings and eyed up the local talent.

'Would you like some coffee?' he offered. 'Or

16

would you prefer tea?'

Jenny chuckled. 'I'd prefer coffee, thank you, Captain Jackson. I'm led to believe the Americans are unable to make a decent cup of tea as yet.'

He started to laugh and his eyes twinkled. 'Just give us time, Mrs Procter, just give us time.'

During the following hour, they discussed how they could show the troops the British way of life. Ideas such as inviting some of them into local households on a Sunday, and putting on baseball matches, to show the Brits American sports, were talked about. During this time, they exchanged a few personal details. Jenny told him about Adam, and his having to leave his position in the bank. She asked the American what he did in civilian life. He told her he was a doctor.

Jenny wondered if this charming man had left a wife and children behind, but didn't feel able to question him too closely after such a brief intro-duction, but when he confessed to having a couple of horses at home, and told her how much he missed riding them, she was delighted. It had been the one thing that had kept her spirits up during these hard times. Near to her home was a riding stable where at weekends she would go and help muck out the horses, as many of the staff were now in the forces, and she would ride out whenever she could, to keep the horses exer-cised.

'Do you have any free time this coming Sunday, Captain Jackson?' she asked.

He looked a little surprised. 'As a matter of fact I have. Why do you ask?'

'How would you like to go riding?'

He beamed at her. 'Are you serious?'

'Absolutely!' Then she explained. 'You will have to do a bit of mucking out first though. Would you mind that?'

'I can't think of a better way to spend my time! Somehow, around horses I can relax completely.'

'I know just what you mean!' she exclaimed. 'I feel exactly the same. It's like gardening, totally therapeutic.' She then gave him her address and directions. 'Can you be there at nine thirty in the morning?'

He said that he could, and they parted company.

As she walked back through the town, Jenny thought what a nice man Captain Jackson appeared to be. For her part she would welcome his company. She didn't mind riding alone, but with him she could show him the surroundings, familiar to her but for the American it would be a new experience and she would review it again – but through his eyes, which would be interesting.

Rusty Dobbs reluctantly pushed back her bed-covers and moaned as she got to her feet. She was seriously hung over! She staggered into the kitchen, poured herself a glass of water and drank thirstily. Her mouth felt like the bottom of a birdcage. She peered into the mirror and grimaced. If this war continued for much longer she would be old before her time. My God these Yanks could drink! Not that there was a great deal of spirits to be had these days in any of the bars, but all the GIs that had shared her bed had always seemed to be able to produce a half bottle of bourbon from their back pockets. She didn't enjoy the sweetness of the liquor – she preferred a drop of gin – but with the shortages, you took what was on hand and didn't complain.

Walking back to the bedroom, she sat on the bed, opened a drawer in the small bedside table and counted her money. It had been a good night! But she was tired. *This is a hell of a way to earn a living*, she thought as she washed her face and cleaned her teeth. But she'd been on the game these past four years, ever since she'd had a row with her mother and stormed out of the house. She'd never returned. Her father had walked out a couple of years before she had, unable to live with his harridan of a wife. He'd signed on with one of the shipping lines just before the war and had jumped ship in Australia. He had written to her and told her what he'd done and advised her to make her own way in life as soon as she was able.

Rusty loved her father and knew he would be horrified if he knew how she made a living. But life on the streets had hardened her. It could be dangerous dealing with strange men who were prepared to pay for sex. The majority were just lonely and wanted a woman, but there were those who had frightened her as soon as they had closed the door to the bedroom, trapping her inside. She had a few scars to show for those times and some very bad memories, which sometimes caused her to have nightmares.

She could have got a job in a factory, at least that was safe, but life would have been so dull. She was a gregarious young woman and loved to party. The war had made many lose their inhibitions, knowing that their life expectancy could be curtailed, and there was a certain air of jollity in people, determined to enjoy themselves whilst they could ... and she was one of them.

Rusty took a hairbrush to her long tresses. The light auburn hair really was her crowning glory. She wore it long and loose, knowing this was how most men liked it. Not for her the victory roll, the most fashionable hairstyle these days. Her clients loved to run their fingers through her locks. Many said her hair reminded them of Rita Hayworth, the glamorous American movie star, which always delighted her.

Once her hair was neat, she decided to take a walk. A look at the shops, and a stroll in the park afterwards, would do her good. She felt she needed to fill her lungs with fresh air before facing the evening and smoky bar rooms, but tonight she wouldn't drink quite so much.

Southampton's town centre had been deci-mated during the blitz, and one-storey shops had been quickly erected on the bombed sites. The windows were full of utility clothes, so called because all pleats, frills and any kind of frippery had been removed to save on material. Furniture was much the same. Plain with no frills.

Rusty gave a cursory glance at the goods on view, but she didn't really need anything at the moment – and anyway, she didn't have many clothing coupons left, which were needed when purchasing clothing. Hats were not on coupons, though, and she took a little time trying on the latest models before making her way to the park.

Although all the park railings had been taken

down to help with the war effort, the local council still maintained the flower beds, which were always a pleasure to see, and now as Rusty walked through, she gazed at the flower display with great delight. At least some things still stayed the same.

She stopped and sat on a park bench, and taking out a packet of Craven A cigarettes she lit one. She drew on the nicotine and blew out the smoke with great satisfaction. She had often been given Camel and Lucky Strike cigarettes by her American clients, but found them much too strong.

'So this is what you get up to during the day.'

Rusty looked up at a GI she knew, who frequented her local pub and was one of her clients. 'Hello, Hank, how are you, and what are you doing here?'

He sat beside her. 'I've got a twenty-four-hour pass, but decided not to go to London this time, so I've been taking in the local sights, like the old walls and the Bargate. They tell me it's a medieval gate that was the entrance to the town many years ago.'

Rusty shrugged. 'Don't know about that, Hank, but it is old.'

'I'm going to find a place and have an English cup of tea as I've yet to discover a decent cup of coffee in the town. Wanna come too?'

'Why not. If we can find a scone too, you'll be having a proper English tea.'

'A what?'

She sighed. Wasn't it enough that she had to service these men without having to educate them too? 'Never mind, I'll explain later,' she said and led the American away.

Two

It was seven thirty when Rusty wandered towards The Grapes pub in Southampton's cosmopolitan Oxford Street. As usual, a mixture of troops from different nationalities walked around, killing time, exchanging stories and dirty jokes, and chatting up the girls, whose gas masks were slung over their arms and who were giving most of their attention to the GIs – looking for Nylon stockings, chewing gum or candy, as the Yanks called chocolate or sweets. A free night out and a good time was on their agenda.

Rusty ignored the many flirtatious remarks sent her way. She wasn't ready to work just yet. She wanted a quiet drink and chat with some of her friends before business began.

'What'll it be tonight, darling?' asked Maudie, the buxom barmaid, as she hooked up the strap of her bra.

'Just a half of bitter, please. I'm thirsty.'

'Not surprised after what you had last night! Bloody hell! You were well on your way when you came in here, then you left to go on somewhere else.'

'Oh, I know, you should have had my head when I woke up this morning.' She grinned broadly. 'But I wasn't so far gone I didn't remember to take the money first!'

Both women laughed raucously. Maudie knew

22

the score. She'd been on the street years before. 'That's my girl!' she said and moved away to serve another customer.

Rusty took her drink and sat away from everyone in a quiet corner and surveyed the scene before her. As yet none of her contemporaries had arrived. At the bar stood a couple of British soldiers deep in conversation, and further along were two French sailors with the ubiquitous red pompoms on their berets, chattering away in their native language – and four American servicemen, laughing loudly.

Rusty watched them with some amusement. She never ceased to be amazed at the exuberance of the Americans. They mostly appeared to have no reticence at all, unlike the British with their emotions bottled up inside – or 'reserve', as it was normally referred to. But, in her line of work, Rusty had long since discovered that beneath that reserve was often a seething lava of emotion. Some of it good – some of it bad.

A couple of her friends arrived and joined her. They exchanged tales of what had happened to them all the night before.

'One of my punters last night was one of them darkies,' said one. 'Nice gentle bloke, kind of shy. He told me if he'd fucked a white woman in the South where he came from, he'd have been lynched!'

The others were horrified. 'Was he serious?' asked Rusty.

'Oh yes, he wasn't kidding.' She giggled. 'I suppose you could say it was a new experience for both of us. Christ, you should have seen the size of him! It frightened me to death.'

'Did you manage?'

'Just about, but blimey, I was knackered afterwards. I took the rest of the night off!'

They continued to chat for a while, then departed to start work.

It was Sunday morning, and Jenny Procter sat drinking a cup of tea, dressed in jodhpurs, ready for her trip to the stables. Through the open window, she heard the sound of an engine and walked to the front door. As she stepped outside, Captain Brad Jackson, driving a jeep, pulled up in front of her.

'Good morning, Mrs Procter, I hope I'm not late?'

She waited for him to get out of the vehicle. 'No, Captain Jackson, you're right on time. Would you like a cup of tea?'

'Do you have any coffee?' He followed her into the kitchen.

'I had an idea you would say that, and I have a percolator ready.'

With a chuckle he said, 'I can see you are a woman who is organized and ready for any eventuality.'

She handed him a cup. 'I do my best.'

Jenny had warned the owner, Beth Harris, a friend of hers, that she was bringing the American and had been told that an extra pair of hands was always welcome. So it was no surprise when they arrived together.

Beth came over to greet them, and Jenny introduced her to Brad.

'Jenny told me she was bringing you. We are always pleased to have an extra man around, as most of ours have been called up.' She held out her hand.

As he shook it, Brad smiled. 'I can't thank you enough, Mrs Harris. I get lonesome for my horses, and I sure miss riding them. Today will be a great treat for me. What can I do for you in return?'

He and Jenny were set the task of mucking out a couple of stables and filling the feed bags after trundling the muck over to an outside field to add to a pile already there.

'Beth sells this off as fertilizer to those who have gardens in the area and to the local farmers,' Jenny informed Brad. 'Nothing is wasted in war time, as I suppose you realize?'

'Well, I've certainly found that out since I arrived,' he said. 'But you must realize, back in the States we don't have the shortages that you do.'

'Ah well.' She laughed. 'America *is* the land of plenty we're told!'

'Mrs Procter, I do believe you are teasing me.'

'Jenny, please – and yes I am!'

'Please call me Brad, and I guess I'll get used to the British sense of humour in time!'

Eventually, their chores finished, they saddled up two of the mounts and rode out of the stable yard into the quiet of their surroundings. It became quickly apparent that Brad was an excellent rider.

It was the best of mornings, Jenny thought as

they rode through a wood. The bluebells were almost over, but the wild aquilegias were blooming, bobbing their heads on their long stems in a gentle breeze, alongside the poppies.

As for Brad, he was at peace with the world. The feel of the animal between his knees made him nostalgic for his home in Denver, Colorado. There, of course, the vegetation was different. Situated at the base of the Rocky Mountains, the terrain was more arid than the pleasant lush green of the English countryside. There were no mountains to be seen here, only the stretch of fields beyond the wood.

'Look!' Jenny called and pointed in the distance.

Following her gaze, Brad saw wild rabbits playing, until a sudden shot from a gun frightened all but one away.

Jenny looked crestfallen. 'Oh, what a shame!' Then she shrugged. 'I know they have to be culled or we would be overrun, but I don't enjoy seeing it happen.'

'You wouldn't approve of my deer hunting then?'

She looked at him aghast. 'How could you?'

'For the same reason. Venison is great to eat, and I imagine you've eaten rabbit before now?'

She started to laugh. 'That's unfair!'

'But true,' he said.

They rode on in silence. Both lost in their own thoughts, enjoying the moment, until eventually they returned to the stables.

Once the horses had been unsaddled and watered, Jenny turned to Brad. 'If you are still free, would you like to come back to my place for lunch?'

'That's really kind; I would love to, thanks.'

They drove back to the house, and Brad helped Jenny alight and then delved into the back of the jeep and took out a cardboard box, following her inside to the kitchen. He placed the box down on the table.

'I thought you could make good use of these few things,' he said, unpacking the contents. There was a packet of coffee beans, tins of fruit, a pack of butter and a dozen eggs. Plus a bottle of wine.

'Oh my goodness!' she exclaimed. 'It looks as if Christmas has come early. How wonderful, thank you so much.'

'My pleasure. The PX stores here are well stocked; we're very lucky.'

'Uncle Sam looks after you well,' she said as she started to put the things away.

He chuckled. 'Nylon stockings seem to be the favourite purchase of my soldiers.'

She smiled at him. 'I wonder why?'

'I think we both know the answer to that. Fraternizing is OK but it brings its own hazards. You know, venereal disease, pregnancies, family problems. It happens during any war. Here in Southampton, in my job, it becomes my problem too.'

She was immediately sympathetic. 'That can't be easy.'

They sat at the table drinking their coffee, discussing the problem.

'You know how it is, Jenny. Men are away from

27

home, knowing they are going into battle, wondering if they will survive a bullet. They are going to enjoy every moment they can.'

'That I can understand – to a point,' she said. 'But no one thinks about the consequences for the woman.'

He leaned back in the chair. 'That's not entirely fair. The women come on to the men, encouraging them. They must be aware of the risks they take.'

'Some of them do, I'm sure, but what about the girl who genuinely falls in love with a GI? What happens to her?'

'That's the biggest problem of all. Some of the guys are already married or are engaged to a girl back home. That can lead to heartbreak.' He looked at her and smiled. 'Anyway, let's forget about that for today. How about I open the wine?'

Jenny rose from her seat. 'What a good idea. I'll start the lunch. Do you like salmon?'

'Indeed I do.'

'Good. Someone gave me two fillets yesterday. We'll have them with some new potatoes and vegetables from the garden.'

They ate their lunch, walked around the garden, and then sat and drank tea beneath the trees before Brad told her he had to go. They walked to the jeep together.

'Thank you, Jenny, for a delightful day. It was the best time I've had since I arrived here. Will you let me take you out to dinner one evening to return the compliment?'

'Thank you, Brad, that's really nice of you. I'd love to.'

'I'll call you,' he said as he got into the vehicle.

28

Jenny watched him drive away. For her too it had been a really good day and she looked forward to talking again to this charming and intelligent man. She didn't envy him his job. She was sure he had many more difficulties to deal with than he had told her. Welfare, in any shape or form, was never easy.

The following morning, Brad was sitting in his office, preparing for the first problem of the day. A company of Negro soldiers had been posted to Southampton, and this had not been without its issues. For the Negros, many who had come from the southern states where integration was either frowned upon or illegal, the freedom to mix with the local girls, to use any bar, eat in any restaurant of their choosing, was really something, and most of them had eagerly taken advantage of the situation. This, of course, had caused problems with the local inhabitants of the town, but even more so with the white American soldiers – in particular with any who came from the south.

Now Brad had to punish two of his troop. One white, the other black. The two men had been fighting in the camp, cheered on by their contemporaries, until the fight had been broken up by the military police.

The duty sergeant marched the two men into the office. Both showed bruises and black eyes from the confrontation. But they stood to attention before Brad, upright and seething with resentment.

He looked coldly at them. 'We are here to fight the Germans, not each other! I will *not* tolerate such behaviour from my soldiers – do you understand?'

'Yes sir,' they answered in unison.

He looked at the white soldier and glanced down at the paper before him. 'You, Private Franklin, are no longer on your home ground in Alabama. You are a soldier in the United States Army, and as such you have a duty to perform. One of which is to uphold the good name of the country for which you serve! Every single one of us will have to face the enemy in the future, and I suggest you keep your anger for that moment. It could mean the difference between life or death.'

He continued: 'Every member of the American forces is pivotal to their company, whatever their colour and creed. Black or white, when you bleed, your blood looks the same. On the battlefield, you may both have to watch each other's back. There is no place, then, to harbour such feelings.'

Then he looked at the Negro soldier. 'And you, Private Nichols, you must think you've died and gone to heaven, here in the United Kingdom. You are no longer restricted by your colour. But that doesn't mean you can behave without decorum, in the town – or here in the camp.'

Brad assigned the soldiers extra duties as a punishment. 'Give me any more trouble and I'll throw the book at you!' Brad warned them. 'Dismiss!'

He was not without understanding for the problems both men faced. Slavery had long been abolished, but in the Southern states, the Negro population still had to sit in the back of the bus – and if it was full, they had to give up their seats to white people. Schools were segregated. For the men brought up all their lives with such rules, the sudden freedom they were given in this country was unbelievable, and Brad could well understand things could get out of hand.

For those white soldiers brought up in the south, to see a Negro walking along the street with a white girl on his arm was intolerable, and the military police had a difficult task, keeping the lid on the situation. There were separate Red Cross clubs for both groups of soldiers, but there were no such restrictions elsewhere in the town.

Brad leaned back in the chair and longed for the tranquillity of the previous day, riding out in the countryside with the delightful Jenny Procter. How civilized that had been, how very enjoyable. What a lucky man her husband was.

Brad himself was unmarried. There had been a girl, but despite his hopes of settling down with her, it had not materialized. When he had been called up, she had backed off, not wanting to be tied down. Now when he thought about it, it had probably been for the best. He picked up a sheaf of papers, ready for the next case.

Three

Sarah Biggs walked through Mayflower Park every morning on her way to work. It was here that German prisoners were kept in an improvised pen. They were a subject of great curiosity to the

31

locals, who would walk by slowly to get a closer look at the enemy.

The first time Sarah had seen them she'd been surprised. Quite what she'd expected, she didn't know, but when she'd looked at the men peering out from behind the wire, they hadn't seemed that different. Apart from their uniforms, of course. Some had glared balefully at her, muttering in German to each other; some had called out; others had taken no notice of her at all.

But one tall young man, with blonde hair and piercing blue eyes, had caught her eye. They'd gazed at one another, and the German had smiled shyly at her. There had been something about him that had intrigued her, and now every morning she looked for him. He always stood in the same place, slightly apart from the others, and he always smiled at her. Sarah would slow her pace and smile at him in return.

One morning he spoke. 'Hello, Fräulein.'

She was startled but secretly pleased. 'Hello,' she replied and kept walking.

The following morning she stopped beside him. 'Hello, are you all right? Are they looking after you?'

He looked delighted. 'Thank you, yes. What is your name?'

'Sarah. What's yours?'

'Gunter Reinhardt. I come from Hamburg.'

And every morning after that they exchanged a few words, until one day he asked if she ever walked in the Park in the evenings.

'Why?' she asked.

'Then we would have time to talk for longer. We

are here from six o'clock for an hour before we are taken to our quarters.'

'How long will you be held here?'

He shrugged. 'I don't know, but I would like to get to know you better before we are moved to another camp.'

And so their strange courtship began.

Gunter told her he was about to study law when he was called up. His father was a lawyer, but he, too, was now in the army, though Gunter didn't know where. He was a quiet young man and Sarah assumed a studious one, from the way he spoke. He had a serious side to his nature, but his smile was warm and she loved the way his eyes seemed to light up when he saw her.

She, at seventeen, was a typist. She told him about her work, her family – her father was also in the army, somewhere in France. They exchanged their plans for the future, though he was somewhat reticent about what lay ahead for him.

'It depends on who wins the war,' he said.

Sarah was certain that Britain would be victorious, but it didn't seem right to say so. They held hands through the wire ... and fell in love.

But when her mother, Dora, found out eventually how her daughter was spending her evenings, she went ballistic.

'Mr James next door told me he's seen you talking to a German prisoner every evening when he comes home through the park. Sarah, how could you?'

'Gunter is a charming young man!' Sarah protested.

'Gunter! Gunter is it? Just how friendly have you got with this man?'

'He's nineteen, not much older than me, and he was called up, just like Dad. It isn't his fault he's in the army. He wants to be a lawyer like his father before him.'

'He's the bloody enemy! Think about it, if he and your father met on a battlefield he would shoot your father without a second thought.'

'And Dad would do the same. It's war, Mother – that's what happens!'

Dora calmed down. 'Yes, you're right, but Sarah, there is no future in it, don't you see? You get too friendly and then he's sent to a prison camp and you'll never see him again. Then how will you feel?'

'Devastated! I love him, you see.'

Her mother was speechless for a moment. 'Don't be ridiculous, you are far too young to be thinking that way. Infatuated, maybe, but love... That's preposterous.'

Sarah stood up. 'I don't expect you to understand – I hardly understand myself – but you can't tell me how I feel. Gunter and I are in love, German or not.' She ran upstairs to her bedroom.

The next morning she told Gunter what had happened. He reached through the wire and took her hand. 'I can understand how your mother feels, *liebling*. Mine would probably say the same. But no matter what happens, who wins the war, we'll be together. Now off you go or you'll be late for work. I'll see you this evening.' He raised her hand to his lips and kissed it.

He watched her walk away, ignoring the coarse

remarks from his fellow prisoners about his friendship with the girl. He hated the war, saw no reason for it. So many people dying – and for what? To satisfy the Führer? A demented man, overcome with a power complex. He had no time for Adolf Hitler, and neither did his father, but now both of them were in the German Army, fighting for a cause they didn't believe in. It angered him that this madman could cause such mayhem and bring death to thousands, just to satisfy his ego.

The only thing that lifted his spirits was Sarah. He counted every minute of every day until he could see her. He dreaded being moved away and wondered if he would be allowed any mail if it came to pass. He wanted to be able to keep in touch with the girl with whom he'd fallen in love. How could they be together in the future? He felt saddened by what seemed to be an impossible dream.

The month passed quickly, and despite the shortages and difficulties that such times can bring, life in the town went on. Jenny and Brad continued to meet at the stables whenever they were free and occasionally met for dinner. Their friendship grew and they slipped into an easy relationship, both learning about one another and appreciating each other. Finally Jenny received a letter from Adam, telling her he was coming home on leave.

As she sat in the garden reading his letter, she had mixed emotions. She was, of course, delighted that he was safe, but during the long time he'd been absent, she'd built a life for herself. She was no longer Jenny Procter, wife of a prominent citizen of the town. She was now Jenny Procter, busy woman, on several committees, doing what she hoped was useful to the war effort. Her work with the American soldiers, she felt, helped both the Americans and the locals to appreciate one another, therefore also helping to keep the peace between them.

Brad Jackson was pivotal in this, of course, and because of their shared responsibility, they had a common interest. Now Adam was coming home on leave for three weeks. Her routine would be upset because he would demand her total attention and would have little patience with anything less. And how would he feel about her spending time with a male friend? Well, he would have to understand that the work she was doing was important, and although she would try and give him as much of her time as possible, he would have to make allowances – like it or not!

Two days later, Jenny waited for her husband to arrive. She was unbelievably nervous. How ridiculous this was, she chided herself as she sipped a gin and tonic to calm her nerves. After all she had been married to the man for eighteen years, although she'd not seen him for the past three. She heard a car toot outside and, taking a deep breath, walked to the front door.

Adam Procter climbed out of the military vehicle and walked towards her.

He had changed, was her first thought. He looked older, careworn and tired.

'Hello, Jenny.' Adam kissed her briefly on the cheek and entered the house; his driver walked behind him, carrying his luggage. 'Just put those down there, Corporal.' Turning back to Jenny, he said: 'I could do with a drink!'

The corporal left, and the two of them walked into the drawing room. Jenny poured Adam a stiff gin and tonic. As she turned towards him she saw that he was looking round the room, eyeing every item of furniture, the drapes at the window, and eventually he walked over to the French doors and looked at the garden.

Jenny joined him and handed him his drink.

'You have no idea how many times I've closed my eyes and tried to picture this room, this view ... and you.'

She was at a loss for words. This was so unlike the man who had left three years ago, and she didn't know what to say.

He turned towards her. 'You look wonderful. How are you?'

Taken aback by a compliment from the man who in the past had seldom noticed what she wore, she said, 'I'm fine, but how are you? Were things really bad over there?'

He crossed to the settee and sat down. 'It was dreadful! I lost a lot of my men during the fighting, which was hard, because in wartime your company becomes your family, so it's like losing a relation. The Germans were better equipped than we were led to believe, so it was a nightmare.'

She sat beside him. 'I am so sorry, but in these three weeks you will be able to rest and recharge your batteries.'

He smiled wearily. 'It's good to be home, not to have to listen to the sound of guns and the whistle of bullets. It all seems very strange ... but wonderful.' He drank deeply. 'My God, that feels good. Now I want to sit in a hot bath and relax.'

This was not the time to remind Adam that he was only allowed a certain depth of bathwater, Jenny decided. She felt he had earned the right to a decent soak.

'You finish your drink and I'll run a bath for you,' she said and left him sitting quietly getting used to his surroundings.

'Darling,' he called, 'would you put out some comfortable civilian clothes for me to change into? I want to get out of this damned uniform.'

So it had started, she thought as she turned on the taps. Why he couldn't sort his own clothes she didn't know, but then, of course, in the past, she had always laid out his clothes for the day, every morning, as he had washed and shaved. So not a lot had changed, really.

Jenny was in their bedroom when Adam climbed out of the bath, and he entered the room with just a bath towel wrapped round his torso. He stood behind her and gathered her into his arms, kissing the back of her neck, caressing her breasts. Breathing heavily.

She shut her eyes and tried not to tense. It had been a long time, and she wasn't sure she was ready for such intimacy. But Adam was.

He removed her clothes with almost indecent haste and pushed her on to the bed. His kisses were demanding, almost brutal in their intensity. She struggled to try and calm him down but he was hell bent on sexual relief.

There was no tenderness in his love-making, and when it was eventually over, Jenny felt as if she'd been used like a whore, rather than as a wife, and she was angry.

She got off the bed, dressed hurriedly and left the room.

Downstairs, she fumed. She would not be used like that again. Only the fact that Adam had just got home, after obviously having been through a great deal, stopped her from venting her anger. She opened the French doors and strode into the garden, walked around it until her anger subsided, then sat on the bench beneath the trees and lit a cigarette. This was where she and Brad often sat after they had been riding, and she couldn't help but compare the two men. Her friend Brad, with his quiet manner and sharp humour, his gentleness and understanding that was no doubt helped by the fact that he was a doctor ... and Adam. She didn't know what to make of him after the scene in the bedroom. There had been no gentleness there. No concern for her and her needs. It had been all about him ... as usual.

She needed to get away. Creeping upstairs, Jenny peeped round the bedroom door and saw that Adam was in a deep sleep. She took her jodhpurs from the wardrobe, changed in another bedroom and went downstairs.

Climbing on her bicycle she rode to the stables and, with Beth's permission, saddled a horse and rode out to the wood. Here among the trees, surrounded by nature, she began to relax.

As she rode, she tried to make allowances for

her husband, attempting in her own mind to picture what he might have been through. It was impossible, of course. She had no idea at all what it was like to be on the field of battle, to see men killed, to feel the fear coursing through you in case you were the next man to stop a bullet.

As she headed back to the stables, she told herself she had to show a little more understanding ... but then so would Adam. After all, she had certain responsibilities, and they were all to do with the war effort. Her way of fighting the enemy, if you like.

Four

The first few days of her husband's leave seemed to be nothing but a whirl of social activity, Jenny thought. Adam, resplendent in his uniform, calling on old and influential friends – re-establishing his place in society.

On the Wednesday, Jenny had promised to meet Brad at the stables to give Beth a hand, and she told Adam she would be out all day.

'That's fine,' he said. 'I'm going to play golf at Stoneham, and after that I'll have some lunch at the golf club with friends. I'll see you back here in time for dinner.'

Jenny arrived at Beth's house and put her bicycle up against the wall. She saw Brad's parked jeep and wandered over to the stable yard, but to her surprise, the American talking to

Beth was a stranger.

'Jenny! Captain Jackson can't make it today but he's sent this gentleman in his place. Wasn't that kind of him?'

The tall, fair-haired soldier smiled at Jenny. 'Corporal Chad Maxwell at your service, ma'am!'

At that moment there was a terrible racket coming from inside one of the stalls. A clattering and a banging, followed by the sound of a horse neighing in fright, filled the air. As they rushed over to see what was happening, one of the grooms hurtled out of the stable, slamming the bottom half of the door shut behind her. The girl was white, and her hands shook.

Beth and Jenny ran over to help her, but the corporal walked over to the stable door, talking softly, trying to calm the terrified animal. Eventually the horse stopped rearing and kicking its hooves against the wall. The three women watched in astonishment as the American opened the door slowly, still talking softly – and entered.

'Is he mad?' asked Beth in horror. 'The PDSA – you know, that veterinary charity – asked me to take the animal, but he's dangerous. I'm going to ask them to take it away or one of my staff could be seriously injured.'

The sudden quiet from inside the stall fuelled their curiosity, and they approached warily. Inside stood Chad Maxwell, stroking the nose of the animal, speaking continuously in his quiet voice. The women watched in fascination as he patted the horse's flanks, then picked up a curry comb and started grooming it.

The steed snorted every now and then, shook

41

its neck and pawed at the ground, but Chad didn't flinch. Eventually, after stroking its nose and nuzzling its neck, he left the stall, closing the door, leaning over the open half – and waited. After a few moments, the horse ambled over to him, snorting softly.

'I know, I know,' said Chad, stroking its neck. 'But things will get better.' He picked up a carrot from a basket nearby, fed it to the animal, then walked slowly away.

Beth followed him. 'I've never seen anything like that in my entire life!' she exclaimed.

'That poor beast has been traumatized,' he told her, 'but I think I can sort him out if you'll let me. I have a forty-eight-hour pass, which would give me enough time to work with him.'

'Of course! What do you need?'

'A place to sleep and the use of your practice ring without too many people around.'

'You've got it!' She looked at Jenny. 'Why don't you take Corporal Maxwell into the kitchen and give him some coffee? That's the least we can do for him.'

Once the two of them were settled at the table with their drinks, Jenny asked the question that was intriguing her: 'Where did you learn how to handle horses in such a manner?'

'I was brought up in Wyoming, and I've been around horses all my life. My dad was a rodeo rider – he used to break horses for a living, and he taught me how to do so at a very early age.'

'But that wasn't just breaking an animal. That was far more!'

He looked bemused. 'When I was fourteen, I discovered this ... gift, if you like. It was like I was able to read their minds, knew what made them tick, what it was that turned them maverick. It just started there and kinda developed. At home they call me a horse whisperer.'

'Amazing!' she said. 'Can I come and watch you work tomorrow?'

'Sure, as long as you don't spook the animal.'

'I promise. When we've finished our coffee, would you like to help me exercise two of the horses? I ride out whenever I can to help Beth.'

'That would be great,' Chad said with a broad grin. 'When this war is over – if I survive, of course – I'm going to buy a small ranch back home and break horses for a living.' He looked wistful. 'I long for the open range, dinner round a camp fire, the peace of the countryside... How about you?'

Jenny sat and thought about her life. Was she content? She had been a bank clerk, which was how she met Adam. Had it been her dream job? No, it was what was on offer at the time and what she'd felt capable of doing. Then had come marriage, and eventually the big house, but no children, which was a great disappointment. She'd never really had a dream. *How sad is that?* she thought.

'I've never lived in a big city, only Southampton. I suppose I'm satisfied with my life as it is.'

He looked intently at her, as if reading her mind. 'I don't think that's true,' he said quietly. 'I think deep down you want *much* more.'

She didn't like to ask him what he meant, but it

unsettled her.

As they rode out Jenny discovered that Chad was good company. He made her laugh with tales of the army, his life on the range and his musings on how strange an English saddle was, as opposed to a Western one.

'You ride well, Mrs Procter, but you need to relax into the saddle more ... like this.'

She did as she was told and immediately felt better. She smiled her thanks.

'There you go,' he said. 'Come on, I'll race you across the field!'

Chad flew ahead of her, and she could see he was at one with his mount and envied his natural talent.

Breathless, she reined in beside him. 'I had no chance!' she protested.

'Of course you didn't, I knew that, but it was fun wasn't it? You should come out to Wyoming after the war – you'd love it. You would feel free; it would be good for your soul. You would blossom, be able to give rein to all those hidden dreams.' He stared at her and smiled. 'You have no idea what I'm talking about, have you?'

Jenny shook her head.

'You will – in time.'

Whilst Jenny prepared the dinner that evening, she couldn't help but relive the extraordinary experience of the day. She'd never seen anything like it. Chad Maxwell was amazing, but also an enigma. The way he'd handled the frightened animal was unbelievable, and then when they rode out together, his insight into her personal feelings was extraordinary. It started her soul-searching. Was she as happy with her life as she thought she was? She realized that indeed she was not. Her marriage was all right; it certainly wasn't perfect, but that was life. After eighteen years with one man, the excitement had long died. She and Adam just went through the motions. Was it enough to sustain her in the years to come? With a sudden realization, she knew that it was not.

At that moment, Adam walked into the kitchen. As he leaned forward to kiss her cheek, she could smell the alcohol on his breath and turned her head away. He hardly noticed as he put his arms around her.

'Hello, darling, did you have a good day?' he asked as he nuzzled her neck.

Oh no, she thought, remembering how he'd used her in bed the previous night ... not again. She eased herself from his hold and moved away, pretending she needed something from the other side of the kitchen.

'Go and freshen up,' she told him. 'Dinner will be ready in fifteen minutes.'

He looked at her through bleary eyes. 'Can't it wait?'

'No, Adam, it can't! It's hard enough to find decent food these days, and I'm certainly not going to spoil it.' She glared at him. 'Fifteen minutes!'

He did not look pleased. 'For Christ's sake, Jenny, I've been away a long time.'

All her thoughts of trying to be understanding flew out of the window. 'I'm well aware of that,' she retorted, 'but that's no excuse to treat me like a whore when you take me to bed.' There, she'd said it.

He was outraged. 'A whore? Whatever do you mean?'

'You didn't make love to me, Adam, you used me. That was the first time and the last. If it's a whore you want, go into town and pay for one!'

His shocked look almost made her smile. She couldn't remember the last time she'd stood up to her husband, and it gave her a good feeling. In three years, she'd changed. Now she was not just his wife, but her own person, and she knew that nothing was ever going to be the same again.

With a feeling of excitement, Jenny cycled to the stables early the next morning to watch Chad work with the maverick horse. He was leading the animal out of the stall when she arrived. The horse was frisky – rearing, snorting and prancing – but Chad just kept talking to it as he led it to the practice ring. With Beth and the female groom, she waited and watched.

Once inside the ring, the American removed the lead rein and let the horse go. It raced around, tossing its mane, rearing and neighing. Chad stood in the centre and watched it. Eventually the animal slowed to a stop, pawing the ground, a wild look in its eyes, ears pricked. Chad sat down and waited.

Beth and Jenny exchanged puzzled glances. What would happen now?

The animal, it seemed, was just as mystified. It pranced and trotted about, then stopped, looked around, neighed loudly, and slowly walked the perimeter of the practice ring, casting the odd glance at the quiet figure in the centre, until it finally stopped still.

Chad rose slowly to his feet. The horse immediately tossed its head and backed up. Staying in the centre of the ring, Chad took a few steps to one side, and after some time the horse moved towards him. Chad retraced his steps, and the animal immediately moved back.

This strange procedure continued until Chad had the animal moving in any direction he required. Progressively the horse calmed down and seemed to be enjoying this strange ritual; it was only then that Chad slowly approached it and stroked its neck, talking softly the whole time. After some time, he walked away, and the animal followed him. When he turned and walked in a different direction, so did the horse. Chad kept this up for half an hour and then finally stopped, his back towards the horse. The animal came slowly closer until it placed its head over Chad's shoulder, snorting softly.

Chad stroked its nose, talking softly as he did so. Then he walked over to the fence and picked up a saddle. He walked slowly towards the horse, talking softly all the time, and very slowly placed the saddle over its back, which unsettled it a little, but Chad just kept talking as he tightened the girth. Then, gathering the reins together, he placed one foot into the stirrup and hauled himself into the saddle.

All those who were watching held their breaths. Chad gave a little pressure with his heels and the horse moved forward. Chad rode him round the ring several times, then he stopped him and changed direction; the animal answered every demand of the rider.

Chad trotted him, put him into a canter, then a gallop and finally a walk, bringing the horse to a standstill. He climbed out of the saddle, stroked the long neck, talking all the time. Then he caught hold of the horse's mane and, twisting it and the neck, eased the horse down on two knees and, ultimately, on its side.

The onlookers were astonished when Chad then sat on the prostrate animal. He continued stroking it, murmuring all the time, until he got off, and he let the animal stand for a moment before leading him – calm, docile and obedient – back to the stall. It was as if he were a different horse entirely.

The three women followed, awed by what they had seen.

When Beth and the groom went about their work, Jenny spoke to Chad. 'That was amazing!'

He smiled at her. 'Not really. An animal is very much like a woman. It thrives on attention, consideration, a firm hand – but above all love.'

Jenny didn't know what to say.

Chad caught hold of her hand. 'All the things that are lacking in your life, I believe, Mrs Procter.'

She gazed into his eyes, eyes that showed no guile, and wondered just what it was about this man that seemed to give him the right to look into her soul.

She removed her hand. 'And if you are correct

... and I do say *if* ... what's to be done about it?'

'That would be entirely up to you. Go away and think about it. We'll talk some more tomorrow. You will be here, won't you?'

'Yes, I'll be here,' she said, then left the stables, somewhat mystified.

When, eventually, Jenny returned home and walked into the kitchen, Adam appeared at the door. 'Where the hell have you been?'

'I beg your pardon?' Jenny's hackles rose at the dictatorial tone in his voice.

'When I woke up you were nowhere to be seen. No note, no nothing!'

'You were fast asleep, and I left early. I expected to be back long before now.'

'Where were you, anyway?'

'I was at the stables watching a man break in a horse.'

His look of astonishment was almost comical. 'You thought that was more important than being with your husband, who has been away for three years?'

Jenny stared at the outraged man before her and thought: *how on earth have we stayed together so long?* Chad's words echoed in her head. 'As a matter of fact ... yes! This man at the stables is extraordinary, and I will probably never see the way he works ever again. It was an experience not to be missed. In fact, I shall be going back to-morrow morning to see him finish his work!'

Adam, for once, was speechless. He stomped around the kitchen, then stopped and looked at Jenny. 'I don't know what's got into you. Ever since I've been home, you've been different. You've changed beyond recognition.'

'Well, I can't say the same for you, Adam! Apart from looking older and a bit more careworn – which is not surprising, under the circumstances – as soon as you settled in you became the same overbearing man who left here three years ago, but now I'm not prepared to put up with it.' Seeing the anger and bewilderment on his face, she did feel some sympathy for him. After all, he had been involved in a war, and he didn't need another one in his own home.

'Sit down,' she said. To her surprise he did so. 'Look, Adam, three years is a long time. I've had to make a life for myself. I belong to lots of committees, I help Beth whenever I can, I *am* a different person.'

'Undoubtedly!'

She ignored this. 'Yes, I am still your wife, and of course I want to spend time with you, but I can't stop all the other things I have to do because you are here.'

He didn't like this one bit. 'A woman's place is with her husband, looking after his needs.'

'I am your wife, not a damned servant!' Now Jenny was angry. 'I have seen to your every need for years – with little reward, I might add! You took me for granted – Jenny do this, Jenny I want that – but now you will have to consider my needs for once!' Having vented her spleen, she capitulated. 'Adam, I am so very happy that you're home, and I do want to spend time with you, of course I do, but we both are leading different lives. That's what a war does to people. We

50

just have to compromise, that's all.'

She gave a half smile. 'In all honesty, I find it strange having you around again. Three years is a long time for us to be apart, you must realize this?'

He suddenly looked weary and, rubbing his forehead, said, 'Of course I understand. As I was driven back here, I wondered how it would be between us. I just wanted everything to be as I remembered, that's all.'

She then realized that he, too, had been un-settled, but in his usual way had hidden his feel-ings. 'Come on, I'll pour us a couple of stiff drinks, cook the dinner, and then we can sit and listen to the wireless. Have a quiet evening on our own.'

Later, when they were in bed, Adam gently took her into his arms and kissed her. Jenny really wasn't in the mood for sex, but after their argu-ment, and because of the fact that he would not be home for long, she responded, even feigning an orgasm to please him. But she was relieved when he kissed her goodnight, turned over and fell asleep.

Five

Gunter Reinhardt was pacing the ground with excitement when Sarah went to meet him that evening. He rushed to the barbed wire fence when he saw her approach and reached out for her hands, gripping them firmly.

'*Liebling!* I have some good news.'

'Whatever is it?' she asked, hearing the urgency in his voice.

'Some of us are being allowed to work outside the encampment. If we are very careful, we'll be able to spend some time together.' He looked at her with longing. 'I want so much to be able to hold you in my arms and kiss you.'

She blushed and lowered her gaze with embarrassment.

'Don't you want that too?'

'Of course I do, but how will it be possible?'

'We are to work in the public park where there is a rock garden. I think it's East Park.'

'Yes, I know where you mean. When do you start?'

'Tomorrow morning. We'll be there all day, I'm told.'

She beamed at him. 'Tomorrow is my half day! I finish at one o'clock. I'll come looking for you.'

'Be careful, *liebling,* there will be sentries on duty, but hopefully by the afternoon they will have relaxed a bit more and forgotten we are the enemy.'

She hated him referring to himself that way. Squeezing his hand she whispered, 'You are not *my* enemy.'

The next afternoon, Sarah strolled along to the rockery area of the park and in the distance saw the men at work. There were only six of them and two British soldiers who were sitting chatting, occasionally casting an eye towards the prisoners of war. She saw Gunter working slightly away

52

from the others and managed to walk in his direction without causing any bother.

He looked up and smiled when he saw her. He glanced over at the sentries, then motioned to Sarah to walk over towards a huge shrub which would shield them from the others. She did and waited, heart pounding, scared of being seen.

A few minutes later, Gunter sauntered round and, with a quick glance over his shoulder, stepped forward and took her into his arms. His urgent kisses took her breath away.

'I have longed to hold you, *liebling,*' he said and kissed her again. 'You feel so good,' he whispered as he held her close and buried his head into her hair. 'You smell so fresh.' His arms held her even closer. 'How wonderful to be able to feel you without any barbed wire between us. But I must go. If they see me, I may never have such a chance again.' He kissed her long and hard, caressed her face, then walked away.

Sarah stood for a moment, catching her breath, her hands shaking. The nearness of Gunter, and the feel of his arms about her and his hot mouth on hers, had been sudden and all encompassing. She walked shakily away and sat on a park bench where she could watch him, longing to be in his arms once more. She would see him again this evening, though the barbed wire would be between them, but at least they could hold hands.

Rusty Dobbs had managed to get hold of an invitation to a dance given by the American GIs at a local hall. She thought she deserved a break and enjoyed getting dressed for an evening's entertainment strictly for herself. She wore an emerald green summer dress covered in white daisies. The green went well with her auburn hair. She wore a pair of silver shoes, hoping to dance the night away.

As she approached the hall she could hear the band playing. Inside, she presented her invitation to the soldier on the door. He looked at her and smiled.

'Good evening, ma'am. Have yourself a good time, you hear?'

'Thanks, I intend to,' she said, laughing.

Brad Jackson saw her arrive. The long auburn tresses first caught his eye, and he watched as two soldiers approached her at the same time. It was obvious to Brad that the men had both asked her to dance, and there was friendly banter being exchanged, with Rusty watching with much amusement. He walked over to them.

'Good evening, ma'am, allow me to settle this argument... Would you care to dance?'

Laughing, she looked at the handsome officer. 'Thanks, I'd love to.'

The two soldiers protested. 'That's not fair, sir.'

Brad grinned at them, patted the bar on his shoulder ostentatiously, and led Rusty to the floor. The band was playing Glenn Miller's 'String of Pearls' as he took her into his arms.

Rusty loved to dance, and fortunately for her the officer was very accomplished – she was delighted. As the music finished, Brad asked her if she would like a drink.

'Thank you, a gin and tonic please.'

He led her to a table and went to the bar. She

watched him and liked what she saw. It was such a treat to be treated like a lady instead of as a sex object, like some of her punters did. Some were polite, others shy, but a few tried to treat her like a piece of dirt beneath their feet, until she put them in their place. She would never let any man disrespect her. If they continued to do so, she returned their money and refused their business. It had caused her a couple of black eyes in the past, but she figured she would have suffered much more had she let them continue. But tonight she was a different woman. Tonight was for her.

She and Brad chatted easily together. She asked how he was settling in England and in the army.

'England is quaint,' he told her. 'You folks are so different, so reserved. We Americans must be a shock to you all. I'm sure we must appear brash and very loud.'

'Believe me, it's a wonderful change,' she assured him. 'I would love everybody to be so open, it's so much fun! You say reserved, I would say stuffy!'

He thought this highly amusing. 'Well, Miss...?'

'Rusty, all my friends call me Rusty.'

'Well, Rusty, you don't appear to be at all stuffy.'

She burst out laughing. 'Dear God, no! Life's too short, Captain. Life is for living, and I don't want to go to my maker without enjoying every moment that I have.'

'Brad, please. Well, Rusty, let's take to the floor again before it gets too crowded.'

Eventually, the band played their last number, and Brad held her close as they waltzed around the floor. As the final notes died, he offered to walk her home.

Rusty hesitated. It wasn't that she didn't still want to be with him, but she didn't want him to see where she lived. She had a small bedsit near Canal Walk, which was by no means a salubrious part of the town. He had treated her like a lady, and she didn't want anything to spoil this illusion. 'Thank you, Brad, but I'll be fine. Honestly.'

He looked concerned. 'At least let me pay for a taxi. It's late, and no young woman should walk these streets alone at this time of night.'

If only he knew how at home she was on these streets at night, she thought. 'Thank you, that would be kind of you,' she demurred.

'How about I take you out to dinner? I'm free on Monday evening. It will be my way of thanking you for tonight.'

'I'd like that very much.'

'Shall I come and pick you up?'

'No, I'll meet you outside the Red Cross club at the Bargate. How about seven thirty?'

'I'll be there,' he said and smiled, then leaned forward and kissed her on the cheek. 'It will give us time to get to know one another better.' He called a taxi, gave the driver some money after Rusty had told him her destination and, with a wave, watched her being driven away.

As she sat in the back of the vehicle, Rusty frowned. This lovely American had no idea that she was a prostitute. How on earth was she to spend an evening with him without revealing too much about her life? He was such a gentleman, well educated, that much was obvious. He had told her he was a doctor in private life, so he probably came from a good background. She was playing with fire, but she told herself that this was war time and people only passed through – nothing was permanent. She dearly wanted to see him again, so she would just have to invent a life that he would find acceptable, she decided. Yes, that's what she'd do, and then she'd enjoy his company until it was time for him to move on. She sat back with a feeling of contentment. Rusty Dobbs, a lady – that's what she would be.

It was Sunday, and Rusty decided to take the day off. She wandered along to the Hoglands where usually the cricket matches were held for local clubs, but today the Americans were playing what to her appeared to be a glorified game of rounders. They called it baseball.

An American GI sat beside her and explained the rules to her as the game progressed. She thoroughly enjoyed the afternoon, as did many of the local children, drawn there primarily in their search for gum and sweets. The soldiers were only too happy to oblige. It was all part of the plan to integrate with the locals, and for all concerned it was a pleasant way to spend an afternoon. Tomorrow, she'd see the handsome captain and enjoy being spoilt yet again.

As arranged, Rusty met Brad outside the Red Cross club by the Bargate. The medieval gateway was a relic of a bygone day which straddled the street and was a constant interest to the foreign soldiers, especially the Americans who had nothing ancient in their country.

Brad suggested they dine at the Polgon Hotel, so they walked past the shops in Above Bar, window gazing. He was astonished when she explained that to purchase any clothes displayed in the window meant that a woman or a man would have to part with clothing coupons also and that there was a limited amount of these.

'You would just love New York, Rusty. You could shop until you dropped with exhaustion. The Big Apple is a woman's dream.'

'I've seen it in American films,' she said. 'It certainly looks exciting, but dangerous.'

'Then you would maybe prefer my hometown in Denver, Colorado.' As they walked he described his hometown and the way of life there. It all sounded so very different to anything she'd ever known. And then they reached their destination.

They sat in the cocktail bar with their drinks, and Brad turned to her. 'So tell me about your life, Rusty.'

She told one lie after another. 'My parents emigrated to Australia before the war, but I didn't want to go, so I got a job as a clerk in an office.'

'Don't you miss them?'

'Of course, but Dad had an offer of a job there and it was an opportunity not to be missed.' And so it went on.

During dinner, Brad listened intently to what she had to say. He thought Rusty was vibrant, beautiful and intelligent, and for the first time in an age he was really interested in a woman. She appeared so confident, so happy in her own skin. She seemed to have no hang ups at all ... and that was refreshing – and she made him laugh.

As they walked back through the town, Brad asked her if she'd like to go to the Red Cross club, but she declined saying it was getting late and she had to get some sleep. But, truthfully, she was fearful that inside the club she might meet one of the GIs who had been a punter and that would have been horrendous.

'Are you sure?' he asked. 'Only, I have to pick up some stuff they have for me.'

'You carry on, Brad,' she insisted. 'I'll go on home.'

'I can't let you do that!'

She touched his arm. 'Of course you can. You'd only have to walk back, and that's crazy.'

'When can I see you again?' he asked.

Rusty was thrilled. She liked this man. 'How about Thursday evening?'

'That's great. What would you like to do?'

'There's a good film on at the Forum cinema I would like to see. I could meet you outside at seven.'

'It'll be my pleasure, Rusty.' He drew her close and kissed her softly. 'Thanks for a great evening.'

'I enjoyed it too,' she told him, then she left.

Just after, she encountered two GIs who were among her regulars.

'Hi, Rusty, what are you doing here? Why aren't you doing your bit for the war effort tonight?'

She laughed. 'Well, boys, I've taken the night off.'

'See you soon,' they said and carried on their way.

She quietly looked up and whispered, 'Thank you God!' How awful it would have been had the two soldiers seen her with Brad! If she continued to see him, life would be fraught with the danger of being found out ... but she was prepared to take the risk. Especially after he'd kissed her. She made a rule that she never allowed her punters to kiss her, it was much too personal. But when she'd felt Brad's mouth on hers, she'd known she wanted more. She wanted to be bedded by a man who was attracted to her, who thought of her as a woman and not a business transaction. But would she be able to fool him that long without being found out? She certainly hoped so.

The next morning, Brad drove to the stables to make his apologies for not turning up the previous Wednesday, but Beth brushed his words aside.

'Please, I can't thank you enough for sending Corporal Maxwell along.' She then told him what had taken place and how the soldier had tamed the maverick horse.

'He was here for forty-eight hours working with the animal, and he came back today to continue. Come with me,' she said. 'Chad has the animal in the practice ring now.'

He followed her, curious to see what was happening. He saw Jenny and walked over to her. 'What's going on?'

'Just watch,' she whispered. 'It's amazing!'

Once again, Chad moved around the ring making the horse turn in any direction he chose. He saddled up and rode the horse around the ring until once again he had the animal laying on its side, where he sat on it. Then, to everyone's surprise, he called the groom into the ring.

The girl looked nervous as she slowly walked towards him.

Chad held out his hand to her and in a quiet, calm voice told her to sit beside him, nearer the neck of the animal. She did so. The horse just raised its head to see what was happening, then lay back down on the ground.

'Stroke him and speak softly to him,' she was told by the American.

The girl leaned forward and stroked the mane, talking all the time. After a while he told her to stand up, and he got the horse to its feet. Chad took a carrot from his pocket and gave it to the girl. 'Feed him,' he said, 'then stroke him, talking to him all the time so he'll get used to your voice.'

Whilst she was doing so, Chad walked over to the fence and picked up a saddle, then walking back he gently put it across the back of the animal, which pricked up his ears, but remained still.

He tightened the girth and told the girl to return to the safety of the fence, then he put his foot into the stirrup and pulled himself on to the back of the animal, talking all the time.

The maverick animal tensed and pawed at the ground, but Chad pulled gently on its mane, then stroked its neck. Gathering the reins, he put pressure on his heels into the side of the horse, and it moved forward and trotted around the ring.

Everyone watched with bated breath as he

urged the animal into a gallop, circling the ring several times, before stopping and beckoning to the groom.

He slipped out of the saddle and held the reins whilst the groom put her foot into the stirrup and mounted, then he handed her the reins.

'Now do what I did. Walk him, then take him into a trot, then a gallop. Try and relax or he'll feel your tension, and don't worry, he won't throw you – not now.'

He stood in the centre of the ring as the girl followed his orders.

The animal responded to her every move. The girl flew around the ring, grinning broadly as she gained in confidence. It was a joy to watch the two of them.

At Chad's signal, she slowed down to a walk and eventually came to a halt. She leaned forward, stroking the horse's neck. 'You good boy!' she said, then she slipped out of the saddle, walked to the front of the animal and stroked its nose.

'You can walk him back to his stall now and unsaddle him,' Chad told her. 'He won't give you any more trouble.' Then he walked over to Beth. 'There you are, ma'am! He'll be fine now.'

'How can I ever thank you?' she said, looking delighted and amazed.

'Well, you can let me come out here when I have a pass!'

With a smile she told him, 'You are welcome at any time.'

Brad looked at Chad. 'Well, Corporal, I had no idea you had such a talent. Well done.'

'Thank you, sir. It was my pleasure, it was like being at home... Well, almost.'

'Come into the kitchen, all of you. I'll make us some coffee.' With this, Beth led the way.

Shortly after, Brad took his leave. 'Sorry, but I have to get back to the office. Good to see you, Jenny. How's your husband enjoying his leave?'

'Very much, thank you.'

'That's great. I'll get back when I can,' Brad told Beth, and turning to the Corporal he said: 'I'll see you back at camp.'

Beth too made her excuses, leaving Chad and Jenny alone.

'You were amazing!' Jenny told the American.

He smiled lazily. 'No I wasn't, Mrs Procter.'

'Jenny, please.'

'I was just doing what comes naturally to me, that's all, Jenny.' He looked at her with his penetrating gaze which she found so unsettling. 'And how are you finding things with your husband home? Are you enjoying his leave too?'

She hesitated just a fraction. 'Of course.'

'No, you're not! You are not enjoying it one bit.'

'What makes you say that?'

'Because you're not happy. You're tense, your back is tight, and there is a certain sadness in your eyes.'

She was speechless.

'Come on,' he said and took her by the hand. 'Let's go for a drive. You need a change of scenery.'

Six

Jenny sat in the jeep beside Chad as he drove to Botley, where he stopped and parked the vehicle. They had travelled in a comfortable silence, despite Jenny wondering why she had agreed to come. She should have returned home by now – although Adam had said he was meeting friends at lunchtime, so he wouldn't be waiting for her, breathing fire at her absence.

She and Chad walked along the peaceful river bank. Apart from a few ducks and a couple of swans, they had the place to themselves. They stopped and sat beneath a tree overlooking the water.

'There are two miracles of nature that bring peace to a person's soul,' he proclaimed.

'And what are those?'

'Water and mountains. Back in Wyoming we have the glorious Rocky Mountains, and lakes of course, but you have no idea what a mountain range can do for your soul. Among them, you can forget everything – except the wonder of nature.'

'You truly are a man of the outdoors, aren't you? I don't think I've ever met anyone like you, Chad.'

His laughter echoed. 'That's because I'm an American!'

'No, it's much more than that. You have an inner peace which is most unusual. You're not in

64

the least egotistical, as most men are.'

He turned his gaze on her. 'Like your husband, you mean.'

It was Jenny's turn to laugh. 'Oh yes. Adam has a huge ego.'

'How long have you been married, Jenny?'

'Eighteen years, although Adam has been away for the last three.'

'That's a long time. People change. You've probably changed more than he has.'

'What makes you say that?'

'Well, it makes sense. Without a man to care for you would have found other things to fill your time. With him away, you were free ... at last.' He continued: 'Within you is a free spirit, Jenny, but sadly it has been smothered during your marriage. Now, having tasted freedom for the first time, you find it difficult to return to your marriage ties.'

'You have an uncanny way of getting into people's minds as well as those of horses. It is very unsettling!'

He found this highly amusing. 'Sorry, I usually keep such thoughts to myself, but I would love to take you to Wyoming because there you could be that free spirit. You could really live the life you want.' He stood up. 'Come on, I think it's time to go home.'

He drove her back to the stables where she could collect her bicycle.

'Would you like me to drive you home? We could put the bike in the back of the jeep,' Chad said.

'No, thank you. I need the exercise. Will I see you again?'

'Oh, yeah, I'll be around here whenever I'm free. You take care, you hear?'

Chuckling, Jenny said, 'You have no need to worry about me, I can take care of myself.'

'I bet you can ... given the opportunity!'

As she rode home, Jenny pondered over the American's words and his uncanny understanding of the human spirit. It was fascinating, but at the same time, somewhat unnerving. She could imagine him back in Wyoming, riding the range, dealing with maverick horses. Well, she wasn't a maverick woman!

The remainder of Adam's leave seemed to fly by. Jenny was busy with committee meetings and keeping her husband entertained, which left no time to visit the stables, and now Adam was returning to his regiment after lunch.

The two of them sat at the table in the kitchen, neither of them feeling at ease with the other now the time had come to part once again. Jenny was wondering when Adam would have his next leave; would he even come through the war alive? She quickly pushed this thought to the back of her head.

Adam sat wondering if the fighting would be as bad as it had been in the past and how many of his men would fall in battle. He gazed across the table at his wife. She had an air of independence about her these days which he found hard to cope with and for a moment he wondered if his marriage would survive this separation. But he immediately thought that once he was home for good things would return to normal, because he would once again be in control and Jenny would no longer belong to so many of the things which these days seemed to occupy most of her time.

He drained his coffee cup, lit a cigarette and suggested they take one last walk around the garden. They eventually sat on the bench beneath the trees. He gazed around the area. 'This is so typically English,' he said. 'I'll carry this scene with me when I get back to France.'

Jenny took his hand. 'You take great care. I want you back in one piece.'

He looked at her with a quizzical expression. 'Are you sure you want me back at all?'

His question shook her. 'Whatever do you mean?'

He shrugged. 'I don't know. It's just that I feel we have drifted so far apart. I seem to have come home to a very different woman from the one that I married.'

What could she say? She was different. She felt different. She also knew that although she loved Adam, she was no longer in love with him. She didn't want to return to the old days, to be at his beck and call. As Chad had said, she wanted much more, and that didn't include her husband ... but she couldn't tell him that, not today of all days.

'It's the war, Adam. Things change, people change, the world changes. When it's all over then everything changes yet again.'

He looked at his watch. 'My driver will be here any moment now.' As he said this, they could hear the sound of a car's engine. They walked into the house and collected Adam's suitcase. At the front door, the driver saluted and picking up the case took it to the car.

Adam put his arms around his wife and kissed her. 'Take care, darling. I'll write when I can.' He hesitated, as if he was going to say more, then he smiled at her and walked to the car.

She watched until the vehicle was driven on to the road. Jenny felt sad. After all, she'd spent so many years with this man, but during the three weeks he'd been home it had been a strain. She'd found it hard to tolerate his dictatorial ways, yet for many years it had been a way of life. She felt confused. What was the future to hold for them, she wondered. Could she continue in this marriage when Adam eventually returned home for good? She didn't think that she could.

Rusty Dobbs was weary. It seemed to her that the troops of all nationalities, waiting to be shipped abroad, had only one thing on their minds – and that was to get laid! During the past two weeks she'd catered for the Americans, the French and a couple of Poles. Language had no barrier when it came to sex. It was take the money, get your clothes off and get fucked! It was as cold-blooded as that. But Rusty was used to that by now. She knew that to become involved further with a punter was a dead loss. A couple of her mates had done so, and the men concerned then wanted their services exclusively – and for free. That was not for her; she was on the game strictly to make as much money as she could, and when the war was over she'd retire from prostitution.

But also during these past two weeks she'd been able to meet with Brad Jackson a few times. They'd been to the cinema, out to lunch and dinner, and they'd once driven to the New Forest to a local pub for a drink. She felt completely at ease with him and enjoyed his company; thankfully, he reciprocated these feelings. They just seemed so well matched, although they came from such different backgrounds. With the exception of having to lie about her family and job, she was able to be herself with him. Apart from liking him as a man, she found him physically very attractive, which was not usual for her, and she was delighted when his kisses became increasingly ardent. The last time they'd met, Brad had told her he had a weekend pass – and would she like to spend it with him in Bournemouth?

He had been so sweet when he'd asked her; he had taken her into his arms. 'At home if I met a girl, I would court her, bring her flowers, candy, spend time getting to know her, but Rusty, in wartime that's not possible. I could be shipped out tomorrow, so I'm being very forward – would you like to spend the weekend with me? I have a weekend pass and would love to take you with me to a nice hotel in Bournemouth. What do you say?'

She smiled as she thought of the concerned expression on his face. He'd been worried that she'd be outraged at such a proposal. 'Why, Captain Jackson,' she had teased, 'are you trying to seduce me?'

'I guess I am. Does that offend you?'

'Not one bit! I told you when first we met, life is for living. I'd love to come with you.'

He looked delighted. 'We'll have to take the

train, I'm afraid.'

'That's fine! Let me know which train and I'll meet you at the station.'

Rusty packed her prettiest underwear and a frilly nightgown with growing excitement. She was going to be made love to by a man she desired and who desired her for herself and not as a prostitute. How marvellous! And to be staying in a hotel, where she would be waited on and cosseted. She could hardly wait.

They managed to sit together, although the trains were busy, not only with civilian passengers but also with so many troops. They chatted away as they passed through the stations, with Brad holding her hand. Rusty didn't give a hoot for the odd glance cast her way by the civilian passengers, who seeing the American uniform were obviously making judgements about her. Whenever she caught one such glance she would smile at the person concerned, who would then look quickly away.

They arrived and took a taxi to a large hotel near the front. Brad signed the register and was given the key to their room on the first floor. In the lift he put his arm around her. 'Hello, Mrs Jackson.'

She grinned broadly at him. 'I am going to enjoy my wifely duties, I think.'

Brad roared with laughter. 'Rusty, you are out-rageous.'

The lift stopped, and stepping out, they found their room. It was spacious, and walking over to the window, Rusty looked out to the sea. Open-

70

ing the French windows, she cried, 'Brad, we have a balcony!'

He stood behind her, looking at the view, then, putting his arms round her waist, nuzzled her neck. 'About these wifely duties... Now or later?'

She turned within his embrace and gently ran her finger across his mouth. 'Now – *and* later,' she said as she kissed him.

Brad picked her up in his arms and carried her over to the bed. He put her down and removed his jacket and tie, then he lay beside her, took her into his arms and kissed her, gently exploring her mouth.

Rusty returned his kisses, running her fingers through his hair, then she unbuttoned his shirt. 'You are wearing far too many clothes, Captain.'

They undressed one another and made love. For Rusty it was like a rebirth. Brad was gentle and thoughtful ... and accomplished. She lay in his arms and for once let her senses run free. She was with a man of her choosing for all the right reasons. Her need for him grew as he explored her body until she cried out for him to take her. He paused only to take precautions, and then he entered her.

Rusty lay back against the pillows, at peace with the world. Her orgasm took her by surprise. She had wondered, as she lay in Brad's arms, if it was possible after so long. She had never done so with a punter and had wondered if she would ever have another. Well, today she had – and it was wonderful.

Brad leaned across her and fondled her breast. 'Let's get dressed and go and find a place to eat.

71

I'm ravenous.'

'Do we have to?' she pleaded, putting an arm round his neck and kissing him.

He looked at her, his eyes twinkling. 'Yes, I think we do, unless you want to wear me out.'

'That's the last thing I want to do.' She chuckled softly. 'I want you to be fit and able to make love to me again and again before we have to go home.'

'You are an insatiable woman!'

'Are you complaining?'

He ruffled her hair. 'Are you kidding!'

They walked along the promenade, went window shopping, and then found a cosy restaurant to have lunch. They chatted and laughed together, both enjoying the secrecy of their new intimacy. It was like being on a honeymoon, Rusty thought. She gazed into the eyes of her new lover and remembered how he looked when he was making love to her, his naked body thrusting himself inside her, murmuring to her, telling her how beautiful she was and how much he wanted her. She reached out to touch him and felt the sexual urgency once again coursing through her veins. As they finished their coffee, she reached out and took his hand. 'Let's go back to our room,' she said softly.

Brad smiled at her, asked for the bill, paid it, then said quietly, 'Let's go.'

The weekend was the happiest that Rusty could ever remember. Brad was a perfect companion as well as a lover. They shared the same sense of humour. They swam, they went dancing, and they walked, talking and laughing together the whole time. Not a moment was wasted.

As they sat in the train on the way home, Brad glanced at the woman beside him, staring out of the window. How lovely she was, he thought. He sat picturing every curve of her body that he'd explored, remembering her little cries of pleasure as he made love to her. But he could also see her cooking his breakfast, being a permanent part of his life, and that made him happy ... but with the war, he'd have to wait before making plans.

As she watched the passing scenery, Rusty knew that when the time came for Brad to be posted, she would be broken-hearted. This man was very special, and she felt so lucky to have been a small part of his life. If only things had been different. She felt she could spend the rest of her life with Brad Jackson and be the happiest woman alive. Meantime, she would just relish every moment they spent together and try not to think too far into the future.

Seven

The latest news of the war filtered through the camp housing the German prisoners, and they didn't like what they heard. In August, the Americans bombed the Messerschmitt works at Regensburg, causing untold damage. For those dyed-in-the-wool Germans who believed in Hitler, it was devastating news; for young Gunter, it was further proof that the war was useless. He now believed that Germany would lose, but he kept those thoughts to himself.

It had been decided by the authorities that if they had to house these men and feed them, then they should earn their keep. Besides, such men with time on their hands could be trouble. With so many Englishmen called to serve in the armed forces, manpower was limited in many areas. Some of the prisoners were escorted to local farmers, who used them to work in the fields. Fields which had been turned into grounds for growing vegetables and corn, to help with the rationing. Others were helping to clear bomb sites – places which had been devastated during the blitz. It soon became the norm to see Germans working for their keep, watched over by armed soldiers.

Gunter had been lucky. He was sent to a small farm, to help the farmer with his cows and pigs, and was allowed to stay with the farmer's family, on the understanding that if he tried to escape, the consequences would be dire.

He was only too happy to comply; anything to get out of the camp. He was able to tell Sarah where he was going, and when he confessed to Mrs Brown, the farmer's wife, that he was in love with an English girl, she allowed Sarah to visit at weekends.

Mr and Mrs Brown took to Gunter, realizing that he was an educated man and not a Nazi. He worked well and was polite and soon became part of the family.

For Sarah, it was a perfect situation. If there

was work to be done when she visited, she stepped in and helped too, which endeared her to the farmers, who were getting on in years. Their son, who would eventually inherit the farm, was away in the army.

Over a meal one Sunday, Mr Brown chuckled. 'If Tim, our boy, knew we had a German working for us, he'd have a bloody fit!'

'Not if he really knew Gunter,' Sarah chipped in.

Mrs Brown looked fondly at her. 'I can only hope that when this war is over, you and Gunter can meet under better circumstances.' It worried the older woman that these two young people, who were so obviously in love, could face great heartache in the future. She wondered just what Sarah's mother thought about the situation.

But Sarah hadn't confided in her mother, knowing how hostile she had been about her daughter consorting with the enemy. Instead, she made excuses when she went to the farm, saying she was with a friend.

During Sunday evenings when all work was finished, Gunter and Sarah would climb into the loft of one of the barns so they could be alone. It was there one evening that Sarah lost her virginity. Being together without restraints of any kind had brought their love affair into the open, and they were able to kiss and cuddle without fear of reprisals, and eventually, their need for each other overcame constraint – and they made love.

As Gunter held her during their love-making, he spoke quietly to her in his own tongue – which didn't bother Sarah, because the tone of his voice was so soft and full of love and passion – and she gave herself to him, willingly.

After, as she lay in Gunter's arms, Sarah knew she wanted to spend the rest of her life with this man and was determined that, no matter what, she would fight for the right.

Brad Jackson had been busy at headquarters and had only been to visit the stables a couple of times in the last few weeks, but he asked Beth if he could bring a young lady over the next weekend. She had immediately agreed, so he mentioned it to Rusty, warning her that they would have to work at the stables, mucking out, but after, they could go for a ride.

'What, on a horse?' she exclaimed, horrified at the idea.

'Of course on a horse.' He looked at her scared expression. 'Don't worry, I'll give you a lesson first. You'll be safe with me, I promise – oh, and wear a pair of slacks.'

She hadn't been really convinced, but Rusty being Rusty, she never turned a new adventure down, and so on the following Sunday morning she drove to the stables with her captain.

Jenny and Chad were already working when they arrived. Brad introduced Rusty to them, and the four stopped for a chat. Rusty told them that she was decidedly nervous.

'You'll be fine,' said Chad. 'Captain Jackson knows what he's doing.'

During the next hour, they cleaned several stables, put down new straw and filled water buckets, and then Brad saddled one of the quieter horses and helped Rusty to mount.

Once on the animal's back, she looked down and said, 'The ground is a hell of a long way away from up here, Brad.'

He put a lead rein on and, trying not to laugh, led the steed away to the practice ring. There he walked the horse around until Rusty began to relax, showing her how to grip with her knees, relax in the saddle and how to hold the reins. After a while she began to enjoy it.

He then told her to gently kick the animal with her heels. She did so and let out a scream as it broke into a trot. 'Oh my God!' she cried. 'How do I stop it?'

'Just relax! I'm on the other end of the rein. Enjoy it, Rusty.'

And eventually she did.

The workforce broke for a snack lunch and gathered beneath the trees. Brad took the horse back to the stable, and then he and Rusty joined them. He'd bought some decent white bread with him and, to everyone's delight, some fresh cheese.

Jenny watched Rusty and Brad chatting away and immediately realized that there was something between them from the intimate looks they exchanged as they talked. She was pleased for Brad; their friendship had grown through their shared work, and she liked the quiet American.

Chad, sitting beside her, also took note. 'It seems as if the captain has found himself a girl,' he remarked. 'That's how two people look at each other when they're in love.'

77

Gazing at them, Jenny had to agree. 'How marvellous, but what happens when Brad is shipped away, what then?' She turned to Chad. 'War breaks so many hearts one way or another.'

He took her hand. 'Not necessarily so. It can also bring great happiness.'

She gazed at the man beside her and recognized the same expression in his eyes as in Brad's. It confused her considerably. During the times she'd met Chad and seen his work she had at first been filled with admiration and awe, but as she grew to know him better, there had been an affinity with him and a physical attraction, which she'd tried to ignore. For one thing he must be at least ten years her junior – and she was married! She told herself that in any case he didn't feel the same, but looking at him now, she knew that he did.

'Come on, let's saddle up a couple of horses and go for a ride, somewhere where we can be alone.' He held out his hand to her, and she took it and stood up.

'We're going to exercise the horses,' Chad told the others, and they walked away.

They rode for quite a while until they arrived deep inside a wood, where Chad reined in his horse, dismounted and tied the reins to a tree. He walked over to Jenny and did the same with her reins, then he waited.

She climbed down from her mount. Chad took a step towards her and took her into his arms. 'I've been wanting to do this from the moment we met,' he said ... and he kissed her.

Jenny lost all her inhibitions when she felt his

mouth on hers, demanding her complicity, which she willingly gave. Never had she felt this way, not even when Adam first took her into his arms, and as Chad led her to a clearing and pulled her down beside him, she gave vent to all the frustration that had built up inside her, surprised at the wanton feelings that flooded her being.

'Oh, Jenny, Jenny,' he murmured as he kissed her. 'You are a wonderful woman, you have so much love in you that has been smothered for far too long.'

She scarcely heard him as she returned his ardour.

They made love beneath the trees in the quiet of the wood, surrounded by the nature that Chad held so dear to him. It seemed a fitting place for her to give herself to this extraordinary man, which she did with great abandon. Never before had she felt free, able to let go of her inhibitions – but with Chad, she was a different person. It was almost like being reborn, and she relished every moment.

After, they lay replete in each other's arms.

Chad gently caught hold of her face and turned it towards him until she was looking at him. 'What are you thinking right this minute?'

'I'm thinking that we have made a lot of trouble for ourselves,' she said quietly, 'but I don't regret a minute of it.'

'Things have a way of working out, honey,' he said. 'We just have to live for the moment – the future will take care of itself. Come along, we best get back before they send out the posse.'

Brad was called away to another camp for a few days, and Rusty returned to her way of life. After all, she had to make a living, and in her mind her world and her love affair with the handsome officer were two separate entities. As long as he didn't find out how she earned her living everything would be fine.

She was sitting in the Horse and Groom in East Street with one of her friends, a place she didn't often frequent as it was the roughest pub in Southampton with a history to match. Most Saturday evenings there was a fight and the police would be called. There'd even been a stabbing and a fatality in recent months, but her friend, another prostitute, worked out of this bar.

It was early in the evening and the bar was quiet, which gave the girls time to chat. They looked up as two GIs walked in. The men strolled to the bar, looked round and seeing the girls asked them if they would like a drink. Before Rusty could say a word, her friend had invited them over.

The soldiers were good company and plied the girls with drink before they got down to business. Rusty eyed the one she would be taking home. Joe was a well-built man, quieter than his friend, but he seemed pleasant enough as they walked down Canal Walk to her bedsit.

Once inside her room he looked around and then at her. 'At least it's clean,' he said and started to undress.

Rusty stopped him. 'Money first, Joe.' She told him how much, and he pulled out his wallet and paid her. As she took her clothes off, Rusty started chatting to him, but he wasn't interested in the niceties.

'I didn't come here to talk!' he snapped. 'That's not what I paid for. Lie down!'

Rusty felt her blood run cold, and warning bells started ringing inside her head, but before she could say a word, the American pulled her on to the bed and held her down. Everything he did was brutal. He held her by the throat, and he pawed at her body, clasping her breast in a vice-like grip which made her cry out with pain. When she complained, he hit her. She struggled against his brute force, to no avail. He hit her again, and she lay still.

The next thirty minutes she thought would be her last as he violated her body. During this time he was silent, which in itself was menacing and terrifying. He took her in various positions, turning her this way and that like a rag doll, until eventually he was satisfied. He then got off the bed, got dressed and, with only a look of disdain cast in her direction, he walked out of the door.

Rusty was unable to move for a while. It seemed to her that every part of her body hurt. She moaned as she tried to get up. She tasted blood from her lip where he'd hit her. As she put her hand to her mouth she could feel the swelling. Tears of anger trickled down her cheeks. 'Bastard!' she cried as she crawled off the bed.

She walked over to the sink in the corner and ran the cold tap, looking at her reflection in the mirror. Her face was now beginning to swell, and she soaked a flannel in the cold water and held it over her face to try and stem the swelling. Putting a dressing gown on she took her toiletries and staggered to the bathroom down the hall, which was shared by the other tenants, and ran a bath. She tried to scrub away every vestige of the brute who had used her so cruelly. As she soaked in the water, she began to cry.

Eight

Rusty felt like hell the next morning. Her face was less swollen, but she was covered in bruises. She silently thanked God that Brad was away because there was no way she would let him see her in this state – how could she have explained? They usually communicated by phone. He told her when to call his office, and that way they were able to keep in touch as she had been careful to keep her address from him and her supposed place of work. Had he been in Southampton at this time, she would have had to make excuses, until her body and face had healed.

Brad had booked them a room in a hotel in Lymington for the following weekend, and Rusty prayed that by then she would be back to normal. She cursed the American who had done this to her and later that day, wearing dark glasses, she met up with her friend from the previous evening, to warn her about him.

'Bloody hell, Rusty, you look as if you've been in the ring with a prize fighter!' said Dorothy when Rusty had lifted her glasses for a moment.

'That bastard took me by surprise. I thought I was a goner, honestly I did. He frightened me to death. I want you to warn all the other girls. That man is dangerous.'

'You should report him to the army; no man should get away with that.'

'What are they going to say? As a prostitute, it's a risk you take. They wouldn't want to know.' Although what she said was true, Rusty knew that if she had made a complaint, Captain Brad Jackson would be the officer to deal with her, so that *wasn't* going to happen, but she didn't share this fact. She'd kept her relationship with Brad a secret from everyone.

Joe Kowalski was not a popular man in his company. He mainly kept himself to himself, but he was known for his vicious temper. A brooding, silent character, he took offence at the smallest thing and had lost many days' pay as a consequence of the fights he'd been involved in. But he was an arrogant man. Today he was having breakfast with the soldier that he'd been with in the Horse and Groom the previous night.

'How did you make out last night, Joe? My girl was great; she gave me a real good time. Worth every nickel.'

Joe swigged down his coffee. 'Mine wanted to talk; I soon put a stop to that.'

'What do you mean?' asked the other warily.

'She was there to service me. That's what I paid good money for, and I let her know it.'

'What did you do?'

'I had to slap her around a bit; she didn't like

83

the feel of my hands on her sweet body. Said I was hurting her.'

The other GI looked worried. 'You didn't do anything stupid, did you?'

'Nah! But I fucked her good and hard, that's what she was there for. I just made her earn her dough, that's all.'

His companion made excuses and left him. He didn't want to get mixed up with anything bad, and he had a feeling that one day there would be a price to pay if he stuck around with this guy.

Joe wasn't bothered by being deserted. He was basically a loner, always had been. He'd been a steel worker in Pennsylvania, like his father. You had to be tough to survive there, and Joe was a survivor. When America came into the war after Pearl Harbor, Joe had seen a way out of his mundane life and signed up. He wanted to see the world, widen his horizons. And now he was in England; next would be France and the fighting. Well, he was used to fighting, and now trained by the army he was a fighting man with a gun and the authority to use it. That suited him just fine.

Rusty rang Brad's office on Friday evening as planned and was told that he had the use of a jeep for the weekend. She arranged to meet him outside the bombed Holy Rood Church at nine thirty on Saturday morning.

'I've really missed you Rusty,' Brad told her, 'I can't wait to see you again.'

'I've missed you too, Captain,' she laughed. 'See you in the morning.'

Saturday dawned, and they set off in bright sunshine with a cool breeze and drove through the picturesque New Forest. Rusty had applied her make-up carefully, as the bruises on her face had faded to yellow, but she still felt sore; however, she laughed and joked with her lover as they journeyed.

When they arrived in Lymington, they checked in to the hotel; but their room wasn't ready so, leaving their bags with the receptionist, they walked down to the harbour and sat on a seat.

Brad took her into his arms and kissed her hungrily. 'God, you taste so good.' And he kissed her again.

'I've missed you too, darling. How did your trip go?'

He sighed. 'War does crazy things to people. The police wanted to take two of the men to court, but I told them the army would deal with them and they would be punished. They caused a hell of a fracas in a pub, and there was no end of damage. They assaulted a couple of the local men. It was a mess. We covered the costs of the repairs, which will come out of the soldiers' pay. They will serve some time in the glasshouse for their trouble.' He smiled tenderly at her. 'What have you been up to in my absence?'

'Nothing much, work and sleep, that's about it.'

He pulled her close. 'Never mind, we have two days to enjoy ourselves. Come on, let's find a place that will make a decent cup of coffee, then we'll take a walk, have some lunch. By then our room should be ready.'

Rusty longed to be in Brad's arms again, but she was worried that in the daylight he would see the bruises on her body that had not entirely faded. 'Wouldn't you rather drive around and see the countryside first?' she suggested, thinking if they made love in the dark, she would be safe from prying eyes.

He looked surprised. 'If that's what you really want to do.'

There was such a note of disappointment in his voice, she gave in. 'No, of course not. I want to be close to you, of course I do.'

'You had me worried for a moment, Rusty darling. I wondered if you had found yourself another man.'

She caressed his cheek. 'Don't be so silly. Why on earth would I want anyone but you?'

They made their way to a nearby cafe, walked along the harbour, had a satisfying meal with several glasses of wine and, after paying the bill, walked back to their hotel.

Once in the bedroom, Brad reached for her. 'Come here, I need to hold you. I feel as if I've been away for an age.'

They eventually climbed into bed, Rusty keeping her underwear on until she was safely beneath the sheets to hide what was left of her bruises. But Brad, caressing her, kissing her, exploring her body, soon discovered them. He looked at her with more than a little concern.

'What the hell has happened to you since I've been away? You're covered in bruises, which by their coloration look to me to be days old.' He waited for her reply.

'I fell over,' she said hastily.

He frowned and stared at her. 'Rusty, you

86

forget I'm a doctor. These bruises are far more than you would have from a fall. To me you look as if you've been manhandled.' He touched her face, which by now had lost the covering of make-up. 'You have the remains of a bruise here too... Rusty?'

She closed her eyes, thinking rapidly, then opening them she said, 'I wasn't going to tell you because I didn't want to worry you, but a drunken soldier attacked me as I was going home from the cinema one night.'

'You reported this to the police, of course.'

'What was the point? I didn't see what he looked like, so what could they have done?'

He cursed beneath his breath. 'Was the soldier British or American?'

'He was a GI. I could tell that much by his uniform.'

Brad looked down at her bare breasts. 'These look like fingermarks!' His jaw tightened and he asked, 'Rusty, were you raped?'

What could she say? No longer could she deny the telltale marks, and in a way she *had* been raped. 'Yes,' she whispered.

He looked appalled, and seeing the tears brimming in her eyes, he held her gently. 'Oh my darling, I am so sorry.' Wiping a tear from her cheek he said, 'What a dreadful thing to happen to you. It must have been terrifying.' He kissed her forehead and tried to comfort her, then he said, 'There is one thing you must do as soon as we go home – you need to go to your doctor and be examined.'

'What for? It's over and done with.'

He spoke very softly. 'You don't know your attacker, but you need to be sure that he hasn't infected you.'

She felt a chill run down her spine. She'd handed Joe a condom when he paid his money, and in the mayhem that followed, she couldn't remember if he'd used it. 'Oh my God!' she cried, now filled with horror.

'It's all right. If by any chance you are, these things can be treated with antibiotics. Trust me.'

Suddenly, her world fell apart, and she broke down and sobbed. 'How can you bear to touch me now?'

He held her tightly. 'Don't be a goose. I love you, I want to take care of you. You couldn't help what happened. Now, Rusty, stop crying, we'll get through this together.'

But of course they didn't make love, and wouldn't until Rusty had been tested, which made her feel dirty. Despite Brad's continued affection and support, their weekend had been ruined.

When on Sunday evening Brad dropped Rusty back outside the church, he drew her into his arms. 'Listen, darling, make an appointment to see your doctor, don't leave it, promise?'

'I promise.'

'Call me in a couple of days. I have to clear a mountain of paperwork, then we'll go out for a meal somewhere.' He saw the uncertainty in her eyes. 'Please don't worry; just remember that I love you.' He drove away.

She walked home, her mind in a whirl. She had

always been so careful about her punters using protection, knowing the dangers of her occupation, but now ... now she was frantic. She wouldn't go to the doctor as there was a special clinic set up in the town. She would make an appointment there. All she could do now was pray.

As Brad drove back to headquarters, he fumed inwardly. If he could only get his hands on the man who had defiled his girl, he would throw the book at him! He pictured her bruised body and tried to shut out the images of what she must have endured. He remembered the fear in her eyes when he suggested she be examined, but he had no choice. As a doctor it was his duty, and as her lover he wanted to ensure her physical being. This girl was very dear to him, and he really couldn't envisage leaving her behind after the war, but these thoughts he'd kept to himself. At some time in the future he was sure to be shipped across the channel into the thick of the fighting, and it didn't do to make too many future plans until the war was over. He would have time then to make his thoughts known.

It was a lot to expect of a woman to leave her country and step into a world that was so different, but he hoped that Rusty loved him enough to do so. In his job, he knew all the difficulties such a move entailed. It wouldn't be easy, but that was life. He could offer her a comfortable existence, a nice home, and he couldn't see why they couldn't be really happy together as long as she was willing to make the move. He chuckled to himself. Rusty's vitality and sense of fun would certainly be a surprise to his family, but he was sure they'd grow to love her as he did.

He visualized her in their home, with guests, friends and colleagues of his, and smiled as he pictured her outspoken ways and imagined how she would see the American way of life. She would find things very different, but he hoped she would come to enjoy them. It would be quite an experience for both of them.

He found the English and their ways quaint, yet there was a certain dignity about the way of life, their reticence, which was rather endearing. It would be something that Rusty, as his wife, could teach to any children they might have.

Nine

Captain Adam Procter sat beneath a tree in the shade, wiping the perspiration from his neck. Sicily was hot! The race for Messina had finally been won by the allies. On August 17th, Messina fell. The allies had captured huge amounts of weapons, fuel and ammunition, but the civilians who emerged from cellars and other hiding places, to see their beloved town flattened, were too distressed to welcome the troops. There were no flowers or wine to greet the conquerors; by now nobody cared.

There were a few cafes and wine bars open, which looked as tired as the local inhabitants –

those who had survived the bombings. But the cost to the American, Canadian and English troops had been high, so they too were weary.

Adam sat and removed the last letter he'd received from his wife. It was now weeks old. Jenny had written to him about her daily life, had seemed to be cheerful, yet he noticed a certain reticence in her writing. It was almost as if she was writing to a friend, not her husband. He couldn't quite put his finger on it, but then she'd changed so much. He put the letter away; he'd write to her this evening when hopefully they would all get some rest.

He sat back and drank his wine as he sat outside the taverna, thankful for the canopy of the huge tree, grateful for the break. How long would it be, he wondered, before the damned war was over and he could return to normal life? War hadn't been quite the adventure he had envisaged. He supposed, like many men, he'd gone into it without realizing what would be asked of him. He'd certainly not been prepared for the carnage he'd seen, the men who'd died, some right beside him. To know he'd been inches from death more than once was a shock to the system.

Jenny, in fact, was enjoying life. Her affair with Chad filled her every moment. Fortunately, he worked for Brad Jackson and was therefore more or less stationary for the moment. When they weren't at the stables, Chad came to the house, and when he had a pass, he stayed the night. The two of them slept together in a guest room, because it didn't seem right to Jenny to take her lover to the same bed she normally shared with her husband.

The difference in their ages only came up once when Jenny mentioned it one evening as they sat curled up together on the large settee. Chad had been dismissive.

'Age is all in the mind, honey. Some people are born old. What to me is more amazing is that a lovely lady like you, from such an illustrious background, could be interested in me, a simple cowboy from Wyoming.'

She had laughed. 'You, Chad, are far from being a simple cowboy!'

His eyes twinkled mischievously. 'If you were to see me on the back of a horse wearing chaps and a Stetson you wouldn't say that.'

'Do you look like Gary Cooper?'

'Hell no, I'm much better looking!'

The situation had not been mentioned since. She just relished the affection that he gave her, the feel of his arms around her at night. The future would sort itself out, and she would enjoy what was on offer from this extraordinary man, for as long as it lasted.

Jenny took the opportunity to show Chad the surrounding countryside and the English way of life, which he found interesting and amusing. They went to Buckler's Hard, where old Elizabethan ships used to be built; to the New Forest, where they both were involved in rounding up the New Forest ponies. This, of course, delighted him.

'Gee, honey, it's almost like being back on the range!' he cried as he whooped his way behind numerous horses being corralled. He was such fun to be with, and Jenny felt free of any encumbrance when she was with him. It was like leading an entirely different life, and she thrived on it ... and it showed.

Beth remarked on it one day when Jenny went along to the stables to help out. After the morning's work had been done and the two women had ridden out for an hour, they returned to the house to eat. They sat in the kitchen chatting about the day.

Beth gazed at her friend with affection. 'Being in love suits you,' she said.

Jenny nearly choked on her coffee, and then she laughed. 'Is it that obvious?'

'Oh yes! You are absolutely glowing, my dear, and you look younger. I'm happy for you; Chad is a lovely man.'

'At first I was filled with guilt,' Jenny confessed. 'I even had dreams of Adam coming home and finding out about us, but as time passed I didn't care any more.' She frowned. 'I just want to be with Chad. Is that so wrong, Beth?'

'You forget, I know Adam and his controlling ways. Over the years he's smothered every bit of spirit in you; now, you are full of life. Grab it with both hands, is my advice!'

'It can't last though; eventually, it all has to come to an end. I can't bear to think about it, to be honest.'

'Then don't! War changes everything, it's inevitable. For you, it's made you happy for the first time in years, and that is worth anything that follows. Come on, there's more work to do.'

Rusty had not been working. She had been to the clinic and undergone the necessary examinations, which made her feel soiled.

The doctor involved was brief and to the point when he was able to give her the results. 'You are lucky, Miss Dobbs. You are free of any infection, but I do advise you to take precautions in the future.' His face was expressionless as he gazed at her. 'It would be a pity if you had to endure this again.'

She felt her hackles rise. 'Do you think I'm an idiot? Believe me, to come here was humiliating enough, and it certainly wasn't my fault that I had to do so!'

His eyes narrowed. 'If you were raped, Miss Dobbs, I hope you reported this to the authorities.'

She picked up her handbag and rose from the chair. 'Thank you for your time, Doctor, you will not see me in here ever again!'

Once outside she leaned against the wall with relief. She didn't dare think of the consequences if the news had been different. Yes, Brad said it could be treated, but she would never have felt the same again. The stigma of having had a sexually transmitted disease would have been for ever carved on her soul. Even now, she wondered if it would affect her relationship with the lovely captain. How did he feel about her being raped ... as he thought? Would he feel differently about her, knowing she'd had sex with another man? Men were strange creatures. They could have sex with anyone they liked, it meant nothing, but if their woman did, well ... that was an entirely different matter. If he ever discovered her profession, that certainly would be the end.

Brad and Rusty sat at a table in the Cowherds Inn and ordered from the menu. It was the first time they'd been together since she'd been tested at the clinic. Brad had picked her up, chatted cheerfully about inconsequential things until they were settled. He leaned across the table and took her hand.

'It's good to see you, darling. You look well. I like your dress.'

'You don't have to be polite, you know!' Rusty was feeling edgy.

'Woah! What brought that on?' he asked with surprise.

'Well, I've been tested; don't you want to know the results?'

He paused and studied her for a moment. Then he said, quietly, 'Yes, eventually, but why are you so angry?'

She closed her eyes and took a deep breath. 'Because I feel humiliated. I'm angry that some bastard used me – and because I'm afraid you won't want me any more!'

Brad stared at her, then, getting to his feet, he said, 'Wait there and don't you dare move!'

The sharpness of his tone so surprised her that she did as she was told.

Five minutes later, he returned, took her by the arm and said, 'Come on, we're getting out of here.'

'But what about the dinner we ordered?'

'I've cancelled it; now get into the jeep.'

He drove down the Avenue into the town, past the Bargate and into the car park of the Dolphin Hotel, where he parked the vehicle, opened the passenger door and said, 'Come on.'

Rusty was so stunned by this turn of events, she went along with him. At the desk, he paused. 'I'm Captain Jackson, I called five minutes ago.'

The receptionist gave him a key.

Taking Rusty by the arm, he led her to the lift and pressed the button for the first floor.

'Brad?'

He ignored her and, when the lift stopped, walked her to a room, unlocked it and gently pushed her inside. 'Come here!'

He took her into his arms and kissed her longingly until she could hardly breathe. 'You don't think I want you any more? Well, my darling, I'm about to prove to you just how much I do.'

To Rusty, the world suddenly looked a much brighter place, and she started to laugh. 'Oh, bloody hell! I've got my own Rhett Butler.'

Brad grinned at her. 'But unlike him, my dear, I *do* give a damn!'

Sarah Biggs and Gunter sat in the garden at the farm at the end of a Sunday, talking about their future. Wondering how much longer the war would take before it was over and the German prisoners of war were repatriated.

'I've not heard from my family, of course,' he said. 'No doubt they have been informed that I am a prisoner, and I have no idea if we still have a home or if it's been bombed during the air raids.' He frowned. 'In fact, I have no idea if my parents are still alive.'

'Oh Gunter, don't say that!' Sarah was horrified by such a thought.

He shrugged. 'I have to prepare myself for this. Both countries were bombed so badly, and there were so many casualties.' He brightened for a moment. 'Maybe if it was bad they might have gone to my grandmother's in the country. Let's hope so. Whatever, *liebling,* we will be together eventually.'

Sarah loved to talk about their future – it was like a dream come true – but the reality of it ever happening was always in doubt. For one thing, her parents would be against it, she knew that for certain. To her mother, the only good German was a dead one! Hadn't she said that often enough? And her father was fighting them somewhere in Europe; she couldn't imagine he would relish a German for a son-in-law. That was only one of the problems that would face them, but at least they were able to be together now; the future would have to wait.

Mrs Dora Biggs had long been suspicious about her daughter's weekends and the fact that she'd stopped meeting the German behind the barbed wire in the park. She knew because her neighbour had told her he no longer saw Sarah there. He'd also informed her that many of the men were now employed on farmlands. Maybe that was the reason, she thought. She decided to find out one way or another. And so the next Sunday, she followed her daughter.

She watched Sarah queue for a bus and take a

seat upstairs. Dora quickly climbed on the lower deck and sat down. Not knowing Sarah's destination, she bought a ticket which took her to the last stop. As they neared the outskirts of the town, Sarah alighted and walked away, and just before the conductor rang the bell, her mother also got off, keeping her distance, making sure she wasn't seen. She had to keep hiding in the hedgerows as there were hardly any people around.

She was surprised when Sarah walked in through the gates of a farmhouse. Dora stopped, wondering what to do. She walked along a bit further where, peering over a hedge, she could see the cow sheds, and to her surprise saw a man in German uniform walk forward and embrace her daughter.

Dora Briggs was horrified and furious. Now she had discovered her daughter's duplicity, she was fuming. *Cunning little bitch!* she thought. Well she wasn't having it. In any case, how could it be possible for an enemy of the country to be allowed such freedom? There didn't seem to be any sentries around. She walked back to the bus stop and waited.

She would go to the council. This wasn't right. Her Sarah was in moral danger; God knows what was going on. It had to be stopped before it got completely out of hand.

Unaware of all this, Gunter and Sarah worked together for the rest of the morning. He tried to show her how to milk a cow, with hysterical results. The cow moved suddenly, and Sarah ended up off the milking stool, on her backside, the pail of milk spilt over her feet.

'Bloody good job you ain't marrying a farmer, lass!' said Mr Brown, who walked into the barn at that moment. 'You'd be hopeless!'

Getting up and trying to wipe away the milk and hay, she had to agree with him.

Ten

Two weeks later when Sarah arrived at the farm on the usual Sunday morning she was met by Ethel Brown, the farmer's wife. 'Come in, my dear,' she said.

The kindly woman looked so worried that Sarah wondered if something bad had happened to her husband. 'Is something wrong?' she asked.

'Sit down, my lass, I'll make us a cup of tea.'

Sarah waited with growing concern.

Mrs Brown eventually sat at the table with her. 'I'm afraid I've some bad news. Gunter has been moved.'

This was the last thing Sarah expected, and she felt as if the wind had been knocked out of her. 'Where is he...? When did this happen...? Do you have an address for him?' The questions poured forth.

Shaking her head, Ethel said, 'I have no idea where he is. Some soldiers came one day, had a few brief words with him, bundled him upstairs to get his things and drove him away.' She paused for breath. 'My husband questioned them, of course, but they gave no explanation, and what's more we won't be having another to take his place.'

Sarah was stunned. 'Did he leave me a message?'

'He didn't even have time to say goodbye; he was as surprised as we were. I can't imagine why they've done this. To me, it's a complete mystery.'

The young girl sat, stunned. How on earth was she to find out where he was? She couldn't sit and do nothing. Gunter and she were going to spend their lives together after the war. They loved one another! Tears filled her eyes. 'Oh Mrs Brown, what am I to do?'

'Well, my dear, all I can suggest is that you go to the military authorities and enquire. I can't think of anything else. You can leave me your address, and then if I do hear anything, I'll let you know. Come on now, have a nice strong cup of tea, it's good for shock.'

Sarah sat on the bus on the way home, absolutely devastated. Gunter hadn't done anything wrong, he'd worked hard, and the Browns had been more than satisfied with his work, so why? Perhaps all the prisoners were to be moved. She had to find out, but she'd have to wait until tomorrow as she doubted the necessary office would be open on a Sunday. But she would take the following morning off and try and discover what had happened. She needed to be able to write to Gunter. He'd be so worried, and he didn't have her address to write to, anyway. The whole thing was a complete mess! She couldn't go straight home or her mother would wonder why she was home so early and start to question her, so she stopped off at Hoglands Park to kill time and watch the Americans playing baseball.

Lots of the GIs were there, and many of the locals who had become interested, even if they didn't understand the rules – and, of course, many young women of the town on the lookout for a free pair of nylons, plus a host of children asking for gum.

Joe Kowalski was also watching, interested in both the game and the girls. He'd caught the eye of one young woman and was chatting to her, teaching her the rules, flirting with her, but when, towards the end of the game, he asked her to go out with him, she refused.

'What do you mean, no?' He was angry because he was sure that he'd scored.

She looked surprised by his response. 'I said no. Besides, I already have a boyfriend.'

'Then what the hell are you doing talking to me?' he demanded.

She retaliated: 'You were telling me the rules of the game, that's all. You bloody Yanks, you're all the same, you think every woman is easy pickings!'

He grabbed her by the arm. 'Now you listen to me, bitch!'

'What's going on here? Let go of the girl, soldier.'

The note of authority in the voice made Kowalski turn. He looked into the face of Captain Brad Jackson.

'Are you all right, young lady?' asked Brad.

The girl wrenched her arm free. 'Now I am, thanks to you.' She glared at Joe. 'You need to teach him some manners!'

As the girl walked away, Brad turned to the GI. 'I want you in my office at oh nine hundred hours tomorrow, soldier – and don't be late!'

'Sir!' Kowalski saluted and turned away, fuming. 'Friggin' women,' he grumbled. 'They give you the come on, then shut you out!'

He was heckled by one or two other soldiers, which didn't help his temper, and he gave them a lot of abuse before he stormed away. He walked to the Horse and Groom, which had just opened, and ordered a beer.

The place soon started to fill up, and he sat at a table watching until he saw a couple of the regular prostitutes enter. The girls stood at the bar and looked around for likely punters whilst they waited to be served. Dorothy, Rusty's friend, was one of the girls, and she immediately recognized the American and quickly whispered to her friend, who cast a glance at the soldier over her shoulder.

Kowalski eyed them both before deciding that he preferred the blonde. He rose from his seat and walked over to the bar. 'Can I get you girls a drink?' he asked.

'No, thank you,' said Dorothy very quickly.

'That's not very friendly,' he said, his eyes narrowing.

'We've just come in for a quiet drink and a chat,' said the other. 'Sorry.' She picked up their two half-pint glasses and the girls left him standing – feeling a fool. This was turning out to be a really bad day, he thought angrily as he returned to his seat.

It didn't get any better. He got into an argument with two British soldiers, who baited him about America not wanting to be involved in the war, happy to let the Europeans take the brunt of the fighting, until they were bombed at Pearl Harbor.

'And now look at you Yanks!' stated one. 'You strut around flashing your money, your nylons, your Camel cigarettes and your gum, thinking you're the answer to every woman's prayer. You can't even march in step!'

The argument became so heated that the landlord came over. 'That's enough! You want to argue? Take it outside or I'll bar the lot of you!'

With a lot of mumbling, the British soldiers moved to another part of the bar and to Kowalski's great annoyance started talking to the two girls he had approached earlier. When, a little later, they all left together, he was furious. He sat until closing time, slowly getting drunk.

When the pub closed for the afternoon, he staggered to the park, curled up under a tree and slept. Three hours later he woke with a raging thirst and made his way to a cafe and had a meal followed by several cups of coffee, waiting for the pubs to open again.

Meantime, Sarah had left the baseball game and walked home. She hardly spoke to her mother as she made a cup of tea before sitting down to read the Sunday papers. But even though she looked at the pages of the newspaper, she didn't read a word. She was thinking of Gunter and wondering how on earth she could find out where he was.

Dora Biggs watched her daughter and saw the

unhappiness etched on her face. She guessed that she was the cause of it but had no regrets. She had to save Sarah from making a fool of herself, it was a mother's duty. One day in the future, Sarah would thank her for her intervention.

Joe Kowalski went on a pub crawl that evening, and with the amount of alcohol he'd consumed earlier that day, he was soon in an alcoholic haze. Joe was never a happy drunk, and already in a bad mood, his consumption only fuelled his temper. He was thrown out of the Lord Roberts, in Canal Walk, and staggered down to the Grapes in Oxford Street, where he ordered a beer at the bar.

'Sorry, soldier, you've had more than enough. I suggest you return to your barracks,' said the landlord.

'Gimme a beer, and less of your mouth!'

'This is my pub, Yank, and you won't get served here. Now leave, or I'll put you out myself!'

The American was enraged. He grabbed an empty beer bottle off the bar and smashed it, pointing the jagged edges at the landlord. 'Come on then. Let's see what you're made of, Limey!'

It was bad timing because, unknown to Joe, two military police had walked into the bar and seen the commotion. They walked up behind him and one of them, using his truncheon, knocked the bottle out of Kowalski's hand. Before he knew what had happened he was handcuffed and bundled into a jeep, cursing loudly.

The next morning, Joe stood before Brad Jackson. He stood to attention, flanked by two

104

military policemen. His head ached, and he felt like hell.

Brad read the report before him; then, looking up, he spoke. 'Kowalski, you are a pain in the butt! You have the makings of a good soldier if it wasn't for your mean disposition and your temper. Being in the army means you must be a team member, but you are a loner. You don't mix with the other men, and when you go out on the town, you make trouble. I saw that for myself yesterday – and now this! God alone knows what you'd be like on the field of battle. My one concern is that you would be out for your own skin instead of helping your fellow soldier, and that worries me. I'm not at all sure I want you in my troop or any other. You are a liability.'

Kowalski's heart sank. Being in the army was a way out from his mundane life. If he was court-martialled he'd have to return to Pennsylvania and the steel works. It was the last thing he wanted. 'Permission to speak, sir?'

'Permission granted.'

'I know I've made a fool of myself, sir, and I apologize. I love the army; in fact, after the war, I'd thought of signing on as a regular. Just give me another chance and I promise I'll be a better soldier and obey the rules.' It cost him a great deal to plead, it was not in his nature to kowtow to anyone, but he *had* to stay in the army – the alternative was too much to contemplate.

Brad saw the genuine concern in Kowalski's face. 'You, soldier, can serve fourteen days in the glasshouse whilst I consider your future. Dismiss!'

Sarah Biggs sat in the waiting room of the local army headquarters the next morning, gripping her hands nervously. She had no idea how she would be received, especially as she would be enquiring about a prisoner of war, but she was determined.

Soon she was ushered into an office and invited to take a seat by the officer sitting behind the desk. 'What can I do for you, Miss Biggs?'

She took a deep breath. 'I am enquiring as to the whereabouts of Gunter Reinhardt, a prisoner of war who was working for Mr Brown at Cherry Tree Farm in Hedge End, but who has now been removed from there.'

The officer looked surprised. 'Why are you interested in this man, miss?'

With a defiant look she said, 'Because Gunter and I plan to marry after the war.'

'Aren't you a little young to be thinking about marriage? And to a German!'

'Gunter and I are in love. It doesn't matter to me that he is German!'

The officer rose to his feet and walked over to a filing cabinet. He admired the young girl's spirit, but personally felt she was wasting her time. During a war, many young women fell for service personnel. It was a known fact, and with heart-breaking consequences mostly, but he would do what he could for her. He sorted through the files and pulled out one, which he took to his desk and read.

Sarah saw the officer frown. 'Is something wrong?'

He sighed. 'It would appear, Miss Biggs, that

your mother complained to the authorities about your relationship with this young man.' He read on and looked up from the papers. 'It seems that you have been visiting Gunter Reinhardt at the farm – is that right?'

'Yes, it was the only way we could meet, but I'm sure my mother didn't know about it.'

He raised his eyebrows. 'According to this report, she did, and she demanded that we put a stop to it. That's why he was moved.'

Sarah was furious. 'How dare she interfere!'

The young man looked at her kindly. 'I'm sure she thought it was for the best.'

'Where is Gunter now?' Sarah demanded.

'I am sorry, miss, but after reading this, I'm not at liberty to disclose that information.'

No pleading from Sarah could make him change his mind, and she left the office in tears. Tears that changed to anger as she made her way home. By the time she walked into the kitchen to face her mother, she was enraged. 'How dare you interfere with my life!'

For a moment, Dora Biggs was startled, then she realized that her daughter had discovered her intervention. 'I had no choice!' she retorted. 'I couldn't stand by and see you get involved any further with this German. Who knows where it would have ended?'

'We were going to get married after the war,' Sarah cried. 'That's where it would have ended, Mother ... in marriage.'

Dora was incandescent with rage. 'Marriage? Marriage to a bloody German...? Over my dead body!'

'That's as far as you can see, isn't it? The fact that he is German, not that he is educated, a gentleman who hated the war. He'll be a lawyer in civilian life, a noble profession, but no, to you he's a German and that's that! Well, let me tell you, I'll move heaven and earth to find him, and you won't stop me!' She stormed out of the house.

Sarah walked to the enclosure were she'd first met Gunter and began to ask the other prisoners if they knew where he was. She had a mixed reception. Some of the men were rude to her, others ignored her, but her pleading reached the ears of one of Gunter's friends. He walked over towards her. 'Are you Sarah, Gunter's girlfriend?'

'Yes, yes, I am! Do you know where he is?'

He walked down the side, away from the others, and she followed on the other side of the barbed wire. 'Can you help me?' she begged.

'I only saw him briefly whilst he waited for transport. He asked me to give you a message if I saw you.'

'Yes?' She waited eagerly.

'He said that when he knew where he was being moved to, he'd write to Mrs Brown and tell her, then she could pass on the address to you.'

'Oh, thank you, thank you so much.' She beamed at him with relief.

'I know that you're both in love and plan to be together after the war. Gunter is a fine man, I hope you make it.' With that, he strolled away.

Sarah was delighted. She'd write to Mrs Brown and tell her the news; then she'd have to wait until the farmer's wife wrote to her with the address. She'd be on pins until she heard, but at least now she had something to cling to. When she knew where he was, she'd go and visit him, but she wouldn't tell her mother. She would never trust her ever again.

Eleven

Brad Jackson drove out to Chilworth for a meeting with Jenny to discuss a forthcoming children's Christmas party to be given by the Americans. Many of the troops were saving candy from their rations towards this end, and Brad wanted to confirm the arrangements.

Jenny opened the door and invited him in. 'It's good to see you, Brad, it's been some time.' She thought for a moment. 'The last time was when you brought your girlfriend over to the stables. How's she doing, by the way?'

'Oh, Rusty's fine. Full of life. She keeps me on my toes!'

They sat in the large kitchen and chatted about the party over several cups of coffee.

'The boys are really looking forward to this shindig,' he said. 'You know how it is, Christmas is a family time, a time for children, and the men feel this even more when they're away from home, so they've put a lot of effort into getting things done.'

She was delighted. 'The children will be thrilled.' A look of disappointment crossed her features. 'I wanted children but it just didn't happen.'

'Did you go to your doctor about it?'

'I did, but Adam refused. As far as I was concerned the doctor could find nothing wrong, and when I told Adam this, we had a fearful row. He accused me of thinking he wasn't a man.' She sighed. 'Oh well.'

'Have you heard from your husband?'

'Off and on, not that he ever has a great deal to say – though you know, with censorship, it's difficult.'

'And what about your relationship with Chad?' he asked softly.

Jenny looked at him for a moment before replying. 'Chad is my guilty pleasure.'

'Your what?'

'You know, when you are doing something you know is wrong but you're enjoying it immensely anyway. That's a guilty pleasure.'

Brad chuckled. 'Well, I've never heard it put into those words before.'

Jenny gazed at the captain. They had become firm friends during the previous months, and she felt she could talk to him. 'Of course, there's always a price to pay, isn't there?'

'What are you trying to tell me, Jenny?'

'I suppose I'm trying to say that, foolishly, I've fallen in love with Chad.'

He frowned. 'Does he feel the same?'

'Yes.' She closed her eyes for a moment, then opening them she looked at Brad and asked, 'What *am* I going to do about it?'

'What do you want to do about it?'

'Oh, that's easy! I want to run away after the war and go with him to Wyoming, ride with him, camp out, sleep beneath the stars, because he makes it sound so wonderful. He makes me feel like a different woman, Brad. I want to change my life ... but I'm married to Adam.'

'Do you still love Adam?'

She shook her head. 'I still love him, but I'm not *in* love with him. Does that make any sense?'

'Oh yes, a great deal. Chad is an unusual man; he's come into your life when you are most vulnerable. Adam's away, you're alone. He's opened up strange vistas, a different way of life. It sounds exciting and probably is – but you'd have to give up a great deal. Are you prepared to do so?'

'I'm damned if I know! The more I try and think about it, the more of a mess it seems to be. Anyway, let's get back to business; sorry to use you as a sounding board, that wasn't fair of me.'

'Don't be ridiculous. I'm your friend, and as a doctor I'm used to listening.'

'You have a great bedside manner, Brad, I'll say that for you!'

'I just don't want to have to treat you as a patient, that's all.' He paused. 'It's possible that in the near future we'll all be shipped out; you should prepare yourself mentally for that.'

Brad knew that plans were in progress for an invasion. There was no way he could tell Jenny about it, of course – it was top secret – but he could warn her of the consequences.

'Wars are dreadful!' she cried. 'Not only do they cost so many lives, but they also mess up the lives of so many of the folk that are left behind.' She rose from her chair. 'I'll make some more coffee.' And the subject was closed.

111

As he drove back to headquarters, Brad thought about Jenny and her predicament, knowing that many couples would be asking the same questions. For him it wasn't so bad – he was a single man, and Rusty was also free. If they wanted to spend their lives together, at least their problems were halved. He had been careful not to speak of the future when he was with Rusty – he didn't think it right to do so with a war still raging – but deep down he knew that in the end he would ask her to be his wife. He loved everything about her. Her personality, her sense of fun – her honesty. He wanted this lovely vibrant woman to share his life, but he would bide his time until things settled down, when he was sure he *had* a future. In war there was always the uncertainty that you could become a casualty – or worse.

Gunter Reinhardt was now settled in a prisoner of war camp at Bishop's Waltham and was not a happy man. It had all happened so quickly. He'd been taken by surprise when he'd been removed from Cherry Tree Farm, and until he'd been taken before the military he had no idea why. Then he was told by the officer in charge – a man not entirely unsympathetic, who realized that Gunter was an educated man who had been drawn into the war against his better judgement.

'It has been brought to my attention that you have been fraternizing with a young English girl, Reinhardt. Her mother is demanding that I put a stop to this.'

So that was what it was all about, thought the German.

'What do you have to say for yourself?'

'It's true, sir. Sarah and I started talking one day when I was being held in Southampton, and when I was moved, she came to the farm on a Sunday. This is far more than fraternizing, sir. We love each other, and after the war we plan to marry.'

The officer looked surprised. 'Well, I can tell you now, that her mother will certainly be against such a liaison. She hasn't a good word to say about you Germans! And I believe that her daughter is a teenager.'

'She's seventeen. I do realize that we have many difficulties to overcome, but we truly want to be together after the war.'

'That's fortunately not my problem,' said the officer. 'You will remain at Bishop's Waltham for the time being – and no visitors are allowed. Dismiss!'

The prisoners were allowed to write letters, and Gunter had quickly written to Mrs Brown and given her his address, asking her to tell Sarah where he was. If he couldn't see her, then at least they could keep in touch.

The postman posted a letter through the door of Sarah's house just as she was leaving for work. When she saw her name on the envelope, she quickly pushed it into her pocket and stepped into the street. Once outside she opened it and was delighted to see it was from Mrs Brown.

Dear Sarah, I've received a letter from Gunter who is now at a camp at Bishop's Waltham. Unfortunately he isn't allowed visitors but can receive mail. He asked me to let you know. I have written the address for you. Love, Ethel Brown.

Sarah breathed a sigh of relief. Gunter still wanted her! She was afraid, despite all his endearments, that once they were apart, he would change his mind about them, and she desperately needed him as she was in a great deal of trouble. Her period was late, and she was afraid she was pregnant. Now more than ever she needed his assurance that they did have a future together because when her mother discovered her condition, Sarah was fearful of the consequences. She would write to him tonight.

Later, Sarah, alone in her bedroom, was filled with trepidation as she penned her letter. What would she do if Gunter, on learning her news, then wanted nothing more to do with her? Whatever his reaction, she would certainly keep the baby, there would be no backstreet abortion for her. She wanted his child, someone to love other than Gunter. There had been little affection in her own childhood. Her parents looked after her well and cared about her, but neither was demonstrative. There had never been any cuddles when she was small, and she'd never seen her father and mother embrace each other. This need for affection had been fulfilled by Gunter, who was gentle and caring. She knew they could be happy together, given the chance. If he still wanted her after hearing her news, she wouldn't let anything stand in her way!

Gunter Reinhardt was handed the letter two days later, after roll call. He walked to a quiet corner of the camp and opened it. After reading the contents, he frowned. My God! What a predicament for Sarah. Her mother was bound to discover that her daughter was pregnant eventually – a woman could only disguise the fact for so long – and then there would be trouble. What on earth could he do to help? He paced up and down, feeling absolutely helpless. There was no one he could turn to for assistance. He lit a cigarette and tried to gather his thoughts ... then he stopped his pacing. Of course there *was* one person he could rely on. He walked to his quarters and sat down to write.

On Friday morning, Sarah saw the envelope on the front doormat and picked it up, her heart racing when she recognized Ethel Brown's writing. She'd heard from Gunter, the farmer's wife wrote, and she had a letter for her. If Sarah would come to the farm on Sunday, she could collect it and stay for lunch.

Sarah could hardly wait. What would her lover have to say about the baby? What if he said he wasn't interested? A million thoughts raced through her mind. If he wanted it and her, how long would he have to wait before they could all be together – and how would she manage in the meantime to keep the child in food and clothes? Her mother wouldn't help, she was sure of that. She was near to tears as she wrestled mentally with all these questions.

Eventually Sunday arrived, and Sarah caught the bus to Hedge End and Cherry Tree Farm. As she walked up the path to the farmhouse, she felt nauseous. Would the letter contain good or bad news? She knocked on the door.

'Come in, love,' said Mrs Brown, and on seeing how pale the young girl looked, she led her to a chair, handed her the letter and said: 'Here you are, Sarah, you read that whilst I make a pot of tea.'

With trembling fingers, Sarah tore the envelope open.

Liebling, it began, *I was so thrilled to hear from you. I had been so worried after I was moved from the farm without being able to let you know what had happened. I love you, Sarah, and although I know the fact that you may be carrying my child will cause you many problems, please know that I am thrilled that we made a baby together.* Sarah let out a muffled cry as she read his words. *I feel so helpless as I am unable at this time to be of any assistance to you, but I have written to Mrs Brown – she knows what is happening and has told me that if she can help you in any way, to ask. I love you, and one day we will be together, I promise. Gunter xx*

With tears of relief trickling down her cheeks, Sarah looked up at Ethel Brown. The woman, seeing her distress, rushed over to her and held her. 'There, there, love, now don't you worry. It'll all be all right in the end, you'll see.'

The two of them sat at the table and, over several cups of tea, Sarah told Ethel she was worried as to how her parents would react when they discovered her condition.

'Are you sure about the baby?'

'I've missed a couple of periods and I'm as regular as clockwork usually,' Sarah told her. 'And another thing, my breasts are tender.'

'Well, sometimes that happens just before you come on,' Mrs Brown remarked. 'However, my dear, I've been thinking after I received Gunter's letter, and I've discussed this with my husband.' She paused to pour more tea. 'Just supposing your mother goes bananas and you want a place to stay, you can have Gunter's old room.'

Sarah's eyes widened with surprise. 'You would do that for me?'

'You and Gunter, yes. Look, love, he was a lovely young man, not the usual soldier. He is a man with a good background, a profession. We grew very fond of him when he was here, and he loves you dearly. He used to talk to Mr Brown and me about his plans for both of you. He had the future all worked out, and he did realize that it wouldn't be easy, knowing how your mum feels.' She sighed. 'Not all Germans are bad, and not all Englishmen are good.'

'If only Mum thought that way, my life would be so easy.'

'If you really are pregnant, when will you tell her?'

Sarah pulled a face. 'Not until I have to, that's for sure!'

'But if you are, you'll have to see a doctor. You must look after yourself and the baby.'

'Yes, I suppose I must.' She frowned. 'To be honest, the only thing I could think about was how Gunter would react when he knew. I hadn't thought further than that.'

Ethel smiled her understanding. 'That's natural. So many young women in wartime are left in the lurch by soldiers who have promised them the earth to get them into bed, but Gunter's different. For that we must all be thankful.'

Arthur Brown joined them for lunch. He was kind to Sarah, as always, but he made no comment about the reason for her being there, except to say how good it was to see her and how they had missed her.

As she left to go home, Ethel Brown said, 'I've suggested that Gunter send his letters for you to the farm only – they are marked with a military stamp, and if your mother saw that, the cat would be out of the bag.'

Sarah hugged her. 'What would I do without you!'

'Ah well, my dear, I'm a sucker for a real love story.' And she kissed her on the cheek. 'See you next week. You take care now.'

As she walked back through the farmyard, Sarah remembered just how happy she and Gunter had been spending their time together here; it had been a great start to their relationship. Being part of a family had seemed so normal. They'd been able to forget the differences between them that the war had only emphasized.

Sitting on the bus heading for home, Sarah felt as if a load had been lifted from her shoulders. Gunter still loved her, and Mr and Mrs Brown had pledged their support. What a lucky girl she was, but she knew that ahead of her was a very rocky road.

Twelve

It was mid December and the day of the Christmas party for the children, held at the Red Cross Club in the High Street. The room was decorated with paper chains and Chinese lanterns. Inside was a spread of food that made the eyes of the invited youngsters widen with surprise. There were spam sandwiches, and hot dogs in fresh bread rolls, baked in the camp. There were sausage rolls, hamburgers, jellies, blancmanges, and small cakes with icing. A twelve foot high Christmas tree, decorated with coloured lights and baubles and lots of tinsel, stood proudly at one end of the room. Three hundred children gazed in wonder at all that was placed before them.

There was a conjuror, a ventriloquist, and a singer who also danced, who had all been hired to entertain the children, and everything would end with community singing. But the highlight of the afternoon, of course, was the arrival of Father Christmas from a specially built fireplace. The children were each presented with a packet of candy, a packet of cookies and some fruit, all given by the Americans from their rations. The children, filled with excitement, didn't realize his: 'Ho, ho, ho,' and chat with each child was in an American accent.

Both Jenny and Rusty had been invited to help out with the children, and they too were carried away with the excitement of it all.

'Just look at that child's face,' said Rusty as a small boy licked his ice cream, clutching an apple at the same time.

'And look at the faces of the men; they are getting as much out of this as the little ones.'

It was true. Several GIs were playing games and entertaining the children, grinning happily as they did so, having a really good time, their efforts well rewarded by the joy on every child's face.

Chad was there too, down on his knees, giving several children piggyback rides. Jenny smiled to herself. Even now he couldn't get away from horses.

Brad walked over to the two women and putting an arm around Rusty said, 'Thanks, girls, you were a great help. I think this party has been a success, don't you?'

'These children will remember today for a very long time,' Rusty remarked. 'In fact, so will I. I've never had a hot dog before!'

Laughing, he said, 'It's part of the American way of life, honey.'

When it was all over and the children taken home, the girls were exhausted. 'Come back to my quarters and we'll all have a drink together,' suggested Brad. He called Chad over to join them.

But as they entered the corridor leading to Brad's quarters, Joe Kowalski, now back on duty, saw them and recognized Rusty and her auburn hair from the night he had paid for her services. He was more than a little surprised to see her being looked after so attentively by his captain, who was followed by the corporal and another classy looking lady.

'Well,' he murmured, 'who would have thought it? Captain Jackson with a hooker!'

As Christmas approached, Sarah was getting increasingly nervous. She was now three months pregnant and was beginning to find it difficult to hide her condition. She knew that it was only a matter of time until her parents were aware of it too. Already, her mother had remarked that her face was fuller and she was gaining weight. Sarah had passed it off as being the result of their wartime diet. So far, her mother had accepted this.

Ethel Brown had loaned Sarah one or two items of her clothing, which were a size larger, to help Sarah disguise her condition, but the farmer's wife was concerned about the future for this girl, of whom she'd grown fond. She'd discussed her fears with her husband: 'Sarah's mother will hit the roof when she finds out that her daughter's pregnant!'

'Well, love, that's understandable, after all.'

'I know, but now is the time that she needs her family behind her. I can't see that happening at all.'

They were soon to find out.

Sarah stepped out of the bath and dried herself. She'd washed her hair too, which had got soaked from the rain that had fallen all day. Just as she put aside the towel and turned to pick up her clothes to get dressed, her mother walked in, as Sarah had forgotten to lock the door.

'Oops, sorry,' Dora began, but as she turned to leave, she saw the telltale swelling of her daughter's stomach and she looked at Sarah in dismay. 'You're *pregnant!*'

Sarah felt the blood drain from her body. She clutched at the bath to steady herself, then she looked up defiantly. 'Yes, I am. I'm carrying Gunter's child, Mother.'

For a moment Dora was speechless, then she began her tirade. 'You cheap hussy! You stand there and tell me you are carrying that German's child – and you have no shame?'

'It's not how I would have planned it, but no, I'm not ashamed. We love one another. He's going to marry me after the war.'

'Ha!' Dora was derisive. 'That's what they all say. You stupid little fool for believing such a thing. You gave yourself to him on an empty promise; well, you'll have to pay the price. What will people say, do you think, when they see you on the street with your bastard in a pram?'

The cruel words cut deep.

Sarah picked up the towel and wrapped it around her. 'It's no one's business but mine and Gunter's. When we get married the baby will be legitimate.'

'You were brought up to be a decent girl, but instead you behave like a tart!' Dora looked at her with disgust. 'You have brought shame on this family. God knows what your father will have to say about this.'

Sarah found her courage. 'I'll get dressed and

come downstairs, then we'll find out!'

Whilst she dressed in her bedroom, Sarah could hear the raised voices echoing from below and her heart was thudding. Now she was really scared. She took a picture of Gunter out of her handbag and held it to her. Then, taking a deep breath, she headed for the stairs.

That evening, Ethel Brown was surprised to hear a knock at her door. She frowned and looked at the clock. Who on earth would be calling now? She walked to the door.

Standing outside, wet and bedraggled from the rain, was Sarah, clutching a suitcase.

Without hesitation, Ethel ushered her inside. 'My goodness, you're soaked. Now sit by the fire, I'll go and get a dressing gown for you, then you must get out of those wet clothes. It's not good for you or the baby.' And she rushed out of the room. She returned and helped Sarah shed her clothes, gave her a towel and wrapped her in a dressing gown, and then sped into the kitchen to make a pot of tea.

When she returned with it all on a tray, Sarah looked at her in amazement. 'You are an extraordinary woman. Not once have you asked me why I'm here!'

Ethel poured the tea. 'It's fairly obvious, love. I imagine that your family have kicked you out once they discovered you were pregnant.' She looked up at Sarah. 'I'm right, aren't I?'

'Sadly, you are.'

'To be honest, Sarah, it's no more than I expected. I'm just so sorry that I was correct. Here, drink this tea, it'll warm you.' Ethel didn't question her, knowing that once Sarah had settled, she'd tell her what had happened.

After a while, she sat and listened to the sad story and was inwardly furious with Sarah's parents for their heartless attitude towards their daughter. She could see that the young girl was upset.

'Now, you listen to me. Gunter's room is all ready. This is your home for as long as you like. Until you leave to get married, if that's how it works out.'

'You believe that Gunter will keep his word?'

'Of course I do. Don't you?'

'Yes, but after listening to my mother, I couldn't help wondering if she was right about him and I was wrong.' She was fighting back the tears.

Ethel leaned forward and took her hand. 'That man idolizes you, and don't you ever doubt him – not for a minute!'

At that moment Arthur Brown walked in. He looked at Sarah and his wife and knew instinctively what had happened. 'Hello, Sarah dear. Moving in, are you?'

'If that's all right with you, Mr Brown?'

'You are more than welcome, girl. Now, how about a cup of tea? It's bloody miserable out there, and I've just delivered a calf.' He grinned at Sarah. 'If when it's your time you get caught out, don't you worry, I'll deliver your calf too!'

It was Christmas Day, and Jenny had invited Brad and Rusty to join her and Chad. The two

Americans had both given Jenny food from the PX stores to help with the Christmas dinner, plus some champagne and wine.

The day was dry and crisp with a hoar frost in the morning. Jenny lit a fire in the drawing room, with a stack of logs at the ready which Chad had chopped a few days earlier. He arrived early to help her prepare.

As Jenny stood at the kitchen sink, washing the vegetables, he came behind her and encircled her waist with his arms. The scent of his aftershave drifted over her shoulder.

'How's my girl?' he whispered.

She turned within his hold and put her arms around his neck. 'I'm fine now that you're here.'

He gave her a long lingering kiss. 'Mmm, that's nice,' he said and kissed her again.

She reluctantly broke free. 'Now stop that!' she chided. 'Or we'll never be ready when the others arrive.'

'We have lots of time, honey. What's the rush?' he teased.

'Chad, behave yourself! Here, you can peel the carrots and parsnips.' She handed him a knife.

He pulled a face at her. 'Slave-driver!'

The aroma from the turkey cooking in the oven filled the room. 'That smells real good,' he said as he worked away. 'Thank goodness I've found a woman who can cook.'

'And if I couldn't?'

'I'd have to look elsewhere. After all, I need a woman who can cook when I'm out working the range.' He smiled softly to himself and said, 'I'll have to teach you how to use a rifle, just in case some marauding Indians arrive at the ranch when I'm out working.'

Jenny looked at him with horror. 'Indians?'

He laughed until his sides ached. 'I'm only kidding! They're all on reservations these days, but you should have seen the look on your face!'

At that moment the front doorbell went, and Jenny left him still laughing. As she let Brad and Rusty in she said, 'You're just in time to save Chad from being murdered.'

'Oh my God, why?' asked Rusty.

'He's been teasing me unmercifully.' And she explained.

The day was one of the happiest either woman could remember. For Jenny, it was being without the constant demands from Adam and the stress of entertaining a room full of people she neither knew nor liked. Of now being held in the arms of the man she loved whilst they all sat enjoying the festivities, eating, and listening to records, and then dancing.

For Rusty, it was being in a nice home, away from the seedy side of Southampton, the pubs and the half-drunken men who were alone and would want to buy her body as a means of bringing some form of comfort to celebrate Christmas. Instead of such a sordid day, she was with a man who loved her for herself. She still lived in fear of being found out, so enjoyed every second she could, with her captain. The man she now knew she loved back and who would break her heart when he left these shores.

At Cherry Tree Farm, Sarah settled down to Christmas dinner with the Browns. It was good to see Arthur Brown sitting enjoying himself, thought Sarah, knowing how long his day was normally. A farmer's life was not easy, but these two lovely people seemed to thrive on it, and Sarah admired their tenacity and enthusiasm.

In her pocket was a long letter from Gunter. He now knew that she was living there permanently. He'd written to say how sorry he was that he was the cause of the break-up of her family, but he'd told her to just think of the family they were starting, together.

I love you with all my heart, liebling. Just think of our future together and of our baby. I just wish I could be with you, but one day we will all be together.

These words would sustain her in the days ahead.

Thirteen

Winter had passed, and the spring of 1944 was upon them. Jenny wondered how the time could have gone so quickly. She heard infrequently from Adam, but so far he was fine. Like so many serving men, all he prayed for was the war to be over so he could return home to normality.

But life was far from normal. Troops and tanks poured into Southampton in preparation for the invasion of Normandy. Code name Overlord. June the sixth the designated day. Men, landing craft and war machines filled every available space. Bulldozers cleared bombed sites to make way for the ever increasing armoury.

Brad was busy, keeping the welfare of the troops in check. Not an easy task, as by now they all felt that something big would happen soon, and they were determined to have a last wild fling whenever they could. Fights broke out in bars between men fuelled with alcohol, wondering if soon they would be dead – and once again, Joe Kowalski, with three other GIs, was up before the Captain. They had been involved in a fracas in a pub with some British soldiers, ending when one of the Brits was thrown through a window.

First up was Kowalski, marched in by Chad and a military policeman.

Brad glowered at the GI. 'I'd hoped I'd seen the last of you, soldier! I see the time in the glass-house didn't teach you a thing.'

Joe didn't answer, but stared defiantly at the captain. He hated being disciplined; he'd had enough of that in Pennsylvania from his father.

'For God's sake, Kowalski, you'll be facing the enemy soon enough, why the hell can't you wait until then?'

Joe straightened his stance. 'I wasn't going to take that crap from no Limey! He was calling us all cowards for not coming into the war before Pearl Harbor. He said we were a shower of lay-abouts, without discipline, only interested in booze and women.'

Brad raised his eyebrows and couldn't help but agree, as far as some of the men were concerned, but he wouldn't give this man the satisfaction of knowing. 'Are you telling me that women were also involved in the argument?' Brad asked, hoping that there were no female casualties as well.

'There were a couple of whores, yes, sir. They wanted to be with us, and the British soldiers didn't like it.' With a sly smile he added, 'You know what it's like, sir. The broads love us Americans, just like your dame. Now *she's* really hot – and very popular.'

Brad froze. 'What are you implying, Kowalski?'

The GI suddenly realized that the captain was unaware that Rusty was a prostitute – this man who'd put him in the glasshouse. What a perfect opportunity to get back at him. 'You mean you get her services for free, when I had to pay? But then you being an officer and all, I expect she gets paid in other ways.'

Chad saw Brad's knuckles clench until they showed white as he fought to keep control.

'Get him out of here until I decide what to do with him!'

As the men marched out of the room, escorted by Chad, Brad took a cigarette out of a pack and lit it. Kowalski must be lying, surely? He couldn't conceive that he was speaking the truth. Not his Rusty ... and yet, there had been a certain ring of truth in the man's voice.

Chad returned to the room. 'Are you ready for the next man, sir?'

'Give me ten minutes, Corporal, then bring him in.'

Outside, Chad took a deep breath. Jesus, he thought, if that GI was right... But he couldn't quite get his head around the fact. He liked Rusty. Could she really be a prostitute? He knew that she and the Captain were real close, he had seen the way they had looked at each other. Whatever would Brad do? He couldn't let the matter rest there; he'd have to find the truth.

How he got through the day, Brad didn't know. He was a professional, so he kept it together, but all the time in the back of his mind was the awful question: was the GI right?

Was Rusty a whore? Had Kowalski paid her for sex? The very idea sickened him. If the man was speaking the truth, how many other men had shared her bed, stroked her body and caressed her – as he had done, but with so much love. This was the woman he'd hoped to spend the rest of his life with if he was spared. Had she lied to him about being a typist? Had *everything* she'd told him been a lie? Surely not! It was driving him crazy. Well, this evening he was taking her out to dinner; tonight he'd search for the truth.

Unaware of the situation, Rusty dressed in readiness for her date. She hummed a tune as she did so. She was deliriously happy. She loved Brad, and he said he loved her too. Never had she thought she'd be lucky enough to meet such a man, and although war was a dreadful time, without it she'd never have met the good-looking captain. Secretly, she wondered if perhaps after the war she and Brad could be together. He had hinted as much without actually committing himself. As he had said, war was full of uncertainties;

until it was over it would be foolish to make plans. She lived in hope, almost too scared to believe it was a possibility. After all, he came from a different class than her, he was a doctor, had been well educated, but happily that didn't seem to make a difference when they were together.

Brad waited for Rusty outside the restaurant where he'd booked a table. His shoulders and neck ached, he was so tense. He lit a cigarette and drew deeply on it to try and bring some kind of relief. He *had* to find out if Kowalski was speaking the truth, but how on earth was he going to broach the subject? He could hardly ask outright: 'Are you a whore?' Besides, he didn't really believe it, not his Rusty ... but he couldn't rid himself of that vague feeling of doubt.

He saw her approaching, saw her face light up as she spied him waiting.

She ran into his arms and kissed him. 'Hello, darling, I'm so happy to see you. Have you had a busy day?'

He answered briefly and ushered her into the restaurant.

As they sat reading the menu, Rusty looked at Brad. She couldn't quite put her finger on it, but something was different. Brad wasn't smiling, he looked so serious. Perhaps something had happened during his working day. She knew that sometimes he had to make decisions that caused him great concern. That was probably it.

They ordered from the menu, and Brad asked the waiter to bring the wine and pour it whilst they waited.

When he had done so, Rusty picked up her glass. 'To us, darling.'

Brad clinked his glass with hers and drank. 'How was your day?' he asked.

She shrugged. 'Same old same old. Letters to be typed, files to be filed.'

'Just where is your office?' he asked. 'You've never told me.'

This took her by surprise. 'Down by the docks,' she said.

'What sort of firm is it that you work for?'

She had to think quickly. 'One of the shipping lines.' She quickly changed the subject. 'How was your day?'

Brad paused for a moment as the waiter served the first course. 'To be honest it was a hell of a day one way and another! Some of my men were involved in a fight at a pub, and one of the British soldiers was thrown through a window.'

'Oh my God! Is he all right?'

'He'll be fine, though he had a few cuts from the glass. He's in hospital with a few stitches. He was lucky. Unfortunately, one of the men involved is always in trouble. A big guy called Kowalski.' He looked at her, waiting to see her reaction. There was none.

Rusty only knew the GI as Joe, so his surname didn't mean a thing.

Brad began to relax. 'The men are all under a great deal of stress, knowing that they'll soon be in the fighting line. All they want is to get drunk and get laid. Business is good for the whores of the town. They must be making a fortune.'

Rusty choked on her food.

Brad stood up and thumped her hard on her back, and then handed her a glass of water. 'Here, drink this.'

She did so, then with some difficulty said, 'It went down the wrong way.' And took another drink of water.

Brad just watched her as she recovered. Was it guilt that had made her choke? He still didn't want to believe that she had been lying to him all this time. He couldn't bring himself to question her further, but neither could he behave normally. His suspicions made conversation stilted, no matter how he tried to be himself ... and Rusty couldn't help but feel the tension between them.

After the meal, Brad made an excuse that he had to return to camp and catch up with some paperwork. He kissed her briefly, put her into a taxi and told her he'd be tied up for the rest of the week so she should call him on Friday evening – and then he went to the nearest pub for a beer.

As she sat in the taxi, Rusty tried to understand Brad's mood during the evening. Yes, he'd had a bad day, but there was more to it than that – his attitude towards her was different. She'd been with him before when his day had been difficult, but he'd always treated her with the same tenderness that had grown between them. Tonight, that warmth had been missing. It was almost like being with a stranger, not a lover. And why all the questions about her work? He'd never been bothered about that before. She just couldn't understand it.

The next morning Brad called Chad into the office. Although they met socially at the stables and at Jenny's, when they were in the office, before other ranks, they maintained a professional outward appearance. Now, however, Chad was the only person who Brad could trust to help him.

'Sit down,' said Brad. 'You heard what Kowalski said yesterday about Rusty?'

'Yes, I did.' Chad wondered what was coming next.

'I want you to find out where he goes usually, what pubs he uses, his general movements when he's on the town.'

Now Chad knew what was wanted of him and why. 'Are you really sure you want to go down this road?' he asked softly.

With a deep sigh, Brad said, 'I have no option. I have to find out the truth or I'll be wondering all the time I'm with Rusty.'

'Look, Brad, you love the girl, it's obvious to everyone when you're together. What if Kowalski is right? How will you feel about Rusty then? The girl is crazy about you, surely you know that?'

'Frankly, at this moment I'm not even sure of my own name!' He shook his head. 'This has thrown me completely. Yes, I do love Rusty; in fact, I had hoped that after the war she'd marry me and move to the States.'

'And now?'

'And now, I'm going crazy.' He looked at the other man, his face grim with worry. 'Could it possibly be true?'

Chad was filled with sympathy. What if it was true, he wondered. It would be terrible. His captain had been so happy with the vibrant woman, and she with him. They looked so right together, and he was filled with trepidation about the task in front of him. 'OK, if that's what you really want, I'll do what I can. But be very sure, because once I leave the room, you'll have started something you may live to regret.'

'No, do it! I won't be able to rest until I know, one way or another.'

Chad rose from the chair. 'Very well. I'll start tonight.'

But, once sitting at his own desk, Chad prayed that Kowalski was wrong. Could he have mistaken Rusty for another woman? No, she was very distinct, with her hair and her exuberance. He couldn't shake the feeling that the GI had sounded genuine. He wasn't just being a smart Alec, and when Brad had queried his comment about Rusty, the soldier had looked surprised. Chad had a bad feeling about what he was about to do. But there was no way he could get out of it. Brad was his friend and had asked a favour of him, so he'd have to do as he was asked. No matter what.

Fourteen

Sarah had just another month to go before the birth of her baby. By now she was feeling heavy and had difficulty sleeping, as the baby seemed to be a night owl and kicked her as she lay in bed. Mrs Brown had advised her to give up work, and when Sarah had said she needed to earn money, the farmer's wife had dismissed her concerns.

'Rubbish! You've been saving, and the baby has a layette all ready. Your stay here and your food doesn't require money; no, lass, you take it easy during these final weeks. The baby will surely benefit, and so will you. You need the rest now, because after you've given birth, you'll be up during the night feeding your child. Anyway, I'll be glad of the company, and you can do little jobs for me in the house.'

To be truthful, Sarah was relieved. She was so tired at the end of a working day, and by now she felt part of the family, which was a great comfort as her own family had disowned her. The Browns had been so good to her, and she welcomed the fact that she could be of some use to Ethel, whose working day seemed long and arduous, so she agreed.

She kept in constant touch with Gunter by mail. They exchanged letters frequently, and last week she'd sent him a snap showing her ever-increasing girth. On the back she'd written: *Your first view of your baby.*

When Gunter received the letter and photo, he took it off to a quiet corner to read and to study the picture. He smiled softly as he looked at the happy face of the mother of his forthcoming child. He ran his finger over her swollen stomach, wondering if he'd fathered a boy or a girl. Then a frown creased his forehead as he realized he might not see his offspring for some time. The future was full of uncertainties. The war was still raging, he was still a prisoner and when event-

136

ually hostilities ceased, he would be repatriated to Germany. Would he be allowed to see the mother and child before he left? And when he was home, what would he find there? Would he still have a home – were his parents alive, would he be able to work? If he had a wife and child, he wouldn't be able to afford to continue his legal studies; he'd have to earn a wage to keep them. He let out a deep sigh. Oh, why was life so complicated and so full of problems?

Captain Brad Jackson was thinking much the same as he waited for Chad to report back to him. When, on Friday, Rusty had phoned as he had requested, he made an excuse, said he was snowed under with work and to call again at the end of the following week. He knew from the tone of her voice that she was disappointed, but at this moment in time, he felt he couldn't face her. He was so wound up about Kowalski's slur on her that he wouldn't have been able to behave naturally, and that would have caused Rusty to question him ... and how the hell could he have explained? No, it was easier this way.

For Chad, too, his task was problematical. He hated what he was having to do. Most of all he dreaded finding out that the GI had been speaking the truth and having to tell Brad, a man whom he admired greatly. It was giving him sleepless nights, and as he tossed and turned one night in the bed he occasionally shared with Jenny, she asked him what was wrong. So he told her.

'Oh my God! I can't believe that of Rusty.'

'I don't want to, but there was something in Kowalski's voice that made me think he was speaking the truth, and that worries me.'

'Oh, Chad, wouldn't it be terrible if it was true? I don't mean so much about Rusty being a prostitute, I mean for Brad finding out. He adores her.'

'And she loves him; it's obvious when you see them together. But I have a bad feeling about this. I wish Brad hadn't asked me to look into it, I really do.'

'If it is true, will you tell him?'

'I don't have a choice, honey. Let's hope I don't have to.'

But a week later, when he had followed Kowalski into The Grapes pub in Oxford Street, Chad's worst fears were realized. He bought a beer and kept himself in the background of the crowded bar, out of Kowalski's sight, and watched. Shortly after, Rusty came into the bar with another woman, and Chad waited to see what would happen.

Kowalski didn't bother them, he was talking to a couple of GIs, but in time, two other soldiers joined the girls, and after a few drinks, they all left together. Chad followed at a distance.

Rusty was laughing and chatting to the American with her, and then they parted from the other couple. Chad followed at a distance and saw Rusty take the soldier into a small house. When he walked up to the door, he could see Rusty's name alongside one of the four doorbells. It was obviously where she lived. That surprised him, as seedy Canal Walk was not the sort of place where a young, respectable typist would live. He waited. An hour later, the soldier came out alone.

Chad walked up to him. 'Gotta light, pal?'

The fellow American stopped and took out a lighter from his uniform and handed it to him.

Handing it back, Chad looked at the man. 'Was she worth the money?' he asked with a forced chuckle.

The soldier grinned broadly. 'I'll say. You want a good lay, buddy, you couldn't do better!' And he walked off.

Chad walked slowly away. He felt sad that in the morning he would have to impart such news to Brad, and he wondered what the consequence would be.

Alone in her room, Rusty put the money she'd earned away in the drawer. She sat on the side of the bed, still in her underwear, and thought: *I can't do this any more.* Every time she took a punter, she felt she was being unfaithful to Brad. She hated it when men pawed at her. Before, it was part of the job, but now it seemed obscene. She walked over to the mirror and looked at her reflection. She ran her fingers through her auburn tresses.

'You need a proper job, girl,' she said. Tomorrow she'd look for something. That American had been her last punter, she decided. From now on she'd be respectable; she owed it to the man she loved.

Chad waited for Brad to arrive in the office the following morning, filled with trepidation. As the captain walked through the door, he stepped forward. 'Can I have a word, sir, before you start the day?'

Brad looked at him and saw the expression on his face, and his heart sank. 'Yes, Corporal, come in.' They walked into his office and closed the door.

Chad stood in front of the desk. He hesitated. 'You asked me to check on Rusty, and I've done so.' He stopped there, hardly knowing how he could carry on.

Brad held his gaze and, with a grim face, asked, 'And?'

Chad gave him all the details; he had no choice. Had he lied, and Brad had discovered the truth later, it would have been worse for the captain.

Brad looked devastated as he listened. 'Thank you, Chad,' he said quietly. 'I know this wasn't easy for you, and I appreciate what you've done. Hold my calls for a while, will you?'

'Yes, I will. I'm real sorry.' He turned and left the office.

Brad sat staring into space, not wanting to believe what he'd heard. How could he have been so easily fooled? How could Rusty declare her love for him when all the time she was taking other men to her bed ... for money! She had lied about her work; had she lied too about loving him? All his hopes for the future died at that moment. And yet ... he still loved her. In his mind he saw her face, heard her laughter, remembered how her soft skin felt as they made love. He got up and walked over to the window, looked out beyond his office, saw people going about their business – and cursed the war.

There was a knock on his door. 'Come in.'

Chad entered and, closing the door behind him, said, 'We don't have anything major to deal with today, so why don't you get out of here? Get some fresh air – it helps to clear the mind. I can cope with anything that comes in.'

Brad looked at him gratefully. 'Thanks, Chad, that's a great idea.'

'No sweat, I'll see you in the morning.'

Brad drove out to the stables and asked Beth if he could take out one of her mounts. She was pleased to see him; she told him which one needed exercising and left him to it.

As he rode out of the stables, he breathed a sigh of relief. Riding, for him, was totally therapeutic; it was just what he needed. He dug his heels into the horse and trotted away towards the woods, trying to clear his mind of the tortuous thoughts that invaded it.

An hour later, he found himself near Jenny's house and rode up the path. He saw her dead-heading the roses in the front garden.

Jenny was surprised when she saw him, and knowing from the phone call she'd had from her lover that his worse fears had been confirmed, she wondered just what Brad was doing here. She waited for him to dismount.

'This is a nice surprise,' she said as she walked towards him. 'Here, tether the horse to this garden post. I'll fetch some water for him,' and she disappeared into the house, emerging soon after with a bucket, filled to the brim.

After the horse had satisfied his thirst she turned to her friend. 'Coffee?'

'Thanks, that'd be great.'

They sat in the kitchen by the window, looking out over the back garden. 'It's so peaceful here,' he said as he sipped his drink and lit a cigarette. 'It's just what I need right now.'

She didn't press him, figuring if he wanted to tell her anything, he would do so in his own time. 'I so enjoy the summer in the garden,' she said, 'because when autumn does come, although it's also a beautiful season, it's a sad one. You know, everything coming to an end before the winter sets in.'

He gazed at her and said, 'I feel pretty autumnal myself right now.'

She waited, and then he began to tell her what had happened. She was silent as she listened, but when he said that the hardest thing to accept was Rusty's lies, she spoke. 'Rusty, for whatever reason, lives a precarious life, and I for one won't judge her, Brad, but one thing I am certain of is that she loves you. That was not a lie; I'd stake my life on it.'

'I'd like to think you're right, but what am I going to do, Jenny?'

She thought deeply as she knew this matter was of the utmost importance; the future of both of them hung on a very thin thread. 'That depends on how deeply you love her and if you can forget the way she earns her money.'

'I find that very hard to do. The thought of other men...'

'You have to talk to her, Brad.'

'And say what?'

'That all depends on you. I can't help you there, I wish I could. But you can't leave things up in the air. You have to sort it, one way or another.'

'Yes, I guess you're right.' He finished his coffee. 'I'd best get back to the stables or Beth will think I've stolen her horse.'

Jenny put a comforting arm through his as they left the house. As he mounted the horse, she looked up at him. 'Good luck, Brad.'

He smiled. 'I guess Rusty was *my* guilty pleasure,' he said. And he rode away.

That evening, Chad drove over to Jenny's house, and they discussed what had happened. She felt so sorry for the doctor who had become such a friend to her. 'Is there anything we can do?' she asked.

Chad shook his head. 'No, honey, Brad will have to work this out for himself. If I was in his shoes, I'm damned if I know how I would react. I feel for Rusty too. OK, she might be a whore, but she's a terrific woman and she's crazy about him... What a mess!'

'I told him that he should see her and get it sorted, but however it turns out, two people are going to be deeply hurt.'

When, on Friday, Rusty rang Brad as arranged, he said he'd be free at seven thirty and he'd pick her up outside Holy Rood Church. He spoke abruptly, which was unlike him. Usually, his voice was full of warmth when he spoke to her, but not now.

'Are you all right, darling?' she asked.

'Yes, fine, just rushed off my feet. I'll see you later.'

As she put down the receiver, she felt her stomach tighten. Something was very wrong. Was he going to tell her he was being shipped out, was that it? It was obvious to all the townspeople that something big was going to happen – you couldn't move for troops queuing alongside the quay and the docks. Armoured tanks were lined up, and the huge Mulberry Harbours being built were now finished. That had to be it, he was leaving!

At seven thirty, Rusty waited outside the church, her heart beating so hard that she almost felt faint. When Brad pulled up in front of her and told her to get into the jeep, she did so.

'Rusty, we need to talk,' he said as they drove off.

Fifteen

They drove in silence. Rusty glanced across at Brad and saw his grim expression, the tightness of his jaw, and she was scared. This man she loved as much as life itself was leaving. By now she was sure this was the reason. What if he was killed in action? She didn't think she could survive such a loss.

Brad headed out through Bitterne and turned off the road towards Hamble, where he eventually parked the vehicle, overlooking Southampton

Water. He switched off the engine and turned to her.

'Whatever is it, Brad?' she asked. But the answer she received shocked her to the core.

'You lied to me, Rusty. You told me that you were a typist with one of the shipping lines, when all the time you were "entertaining the troops"!'

She felt the blood drain from her body. 'Oh my God!' The words escaped her lips before she was aware of them.

'Is that all you have to say to me?' Brad's voice was like ice.

She was stunned into silence. With trembling fingers, she reached into her handbag for a cigarette and lit it, trying to think what she could say. Taking a deep drag on the cigarette, she blew out the smoke and then stared straight into his eyes.

'What can I say? It's the truth. When we first met it didn't matter, we were just having a good time, but when I fell in love with you, I couldn't tell you in case I lost you.'

His eyes glittered with anger. 'You say you fell in love with me, but you still continued in your profession! You didn't love me enough to stop you taking other men to your bed.'

How could she explain? The fact that she had now stopped, and had found a job this week, seemed irrelevant. He would wonder why she had waited so long to do so. Indeed, she wondered that herself.

'I'm so sorry, Brad.'

'You lied to me. Did you lie about your parents too?'

She nodded. 'My father left my mother just

before the war, though he *is* in Australia. Mum lives in Southampton. I left home after a row and I've not seen her since.' She saw the disappointment on his face. 'I wanted to impress you,' she cried.

'Why, for God's sake?'

'Because you come from a much better class than me. I wanted you to think well of me because I liked you – then I loved you. And that isn't a lie, Brad.'

He shook his head as he looked at her. 'Oh Rusty, class wasn't at all important. There was no need for all this subterfuge.'

She gave a bitter laugh. 'Oh really! My mother is a drunk! What's to be proud of?'

'Alcoholism is an illness, it isn't her fault. I've dealt with that in my practice, I know.'

'Have you dealt with prostitution too?' She glared at him defiantly.

'What made you become a prostitute, if I may ask? I'm trying to understand. Why that and not some other job?'

There was no way she could make him understand; it would sound so shallow. How could she tell him she had just wanted a good time and the opportunity arose one night and she just carried on from there, knowing she could make a mint of money?'

'It really doesn't matter why, Brad. I am what I am, and no one can change that.'

He was at a loss to know what to say, as his own feelings were in turmoil. He started the jeep's engine, reversed, turned and drove back to the town.

Rusty sat beside him, tears brimming in her eyes, knowing she'd lost the man who meant everything to her.

Brad stopped the vehicle outside the church where he'd met her. He didn't know what to say. He just looked at her.

She saw the pain etched on his face, and her heart was breaking. She touched his hand. 'I am *so* sorry. I wish it was a different story because I love you so very much.' She leaned forward and kissed his lips softly ... then got out of the jeep and ran down the street.

Brad wanted to call after her, but he couldn't bring himself to do so. He put the car into gear and drove back to the camp.

During the next few weeks, Brad hardly had time to draw breath, which was his saving grace. Overlord was on, and D-Day was approaching. Southampton was packed with troops, lining up ready to cross the English Chanel to Normandy. The weather was bad, and Eisenhower had delayed the crossing for twenty-four hours.

Despite asking his commanding officer if he could be allowed to cross with his men, this had been denied. He was pivotal to the organization, he was told. 'We need you here.' He had to remain in the war room, surrounded by maps, with the plans for the invasion before him.

But when it was time for his men to leave, he spoke briefly to them and wished them luck. As he watched them march out of the camp gates, he wondered just how many would be coming back. He saw Kowalski marching past. He wasn't unhappy to see the last of the man.

Kowalski saw the captain watching and smirked to himself. *Well, Captain,* he thought, *you got what was coming to you.*

But the GI got his as he stepped off the landing craft. He didn't even make the beach, as a single bullet caught him right between the eyes.

Rusty, now working as a shop assistant in Edwin Jones, wondered if Brad was among the troops that were marching through the streets. She was leading a very quiet life these days. She'd moved out of Canal Walk and was renting a small flat in the Polygon area, well away from the streets where she used to trade. Not a day passed that she didn't think of her lover and wish that things could have been different. If only she could have seen him just once more... Remembering how hurt he'd been, it was perhaps for the best, but she was deeply unhappy.

To her surprise, one day in mid June she looked up as a customer paused in front of her counter and saw it was Jenny. She didn't know what to do or how Jenny would be towards her, knowing that she was such a good friend of Brad's.

'Rusty!' said Jenny. 'How lovely to see you. How are you?'

With some relief, Rusty smiled back. 'I'm fine, how are you?'

They chatted about inconsequential things, and then Jenny asked, 'Do you get a break for lunch?'

'Yes, in about half an hour.'

'Good, let's go and get a sandwich together.'

She saw Rusty hesitate. 'Please, I'd like to talk to you.'

They agreed to meet outside.

Once they were settled in a coffee shop and had ordered, Jenny turned to Rusty. 'I am so sorry to hear about you and Brad.' It was said with such sincerity that Rusty was taken by surprise.

'Well, so am I. But what could you expect?' She gazed at Jenny and decided it was useless to pretend. 'You know the reason why?'

'Yes, I do, but who am I to judge you, Rusty? After all, here I am, a married woman, having an affair!'

'Have you seen Brad? Has he been sent to France?'

'No, he's still at headquarters. I've seen him only once, he's been so busy since the invasion, but I can tell you he's not a happy man. He truly loved you, you know.'

'If only I'd stopped taking punters sooner, when I fell in love with him, but it's too late for regrets.' She pursed her lips. 'I am now working in a respectable job, as you saw. I've put my other life behind me, but it's too late for me and Brad. Oh, Jenny, if only I could turn back the clock.'

Seeing the unhappiness in the other woman's face only made Jenny wish there was something she could do.

'How's Chad?'

Jenny smiled. 'He's fine – busy, of course, because he works in Brad's office, but we meet when we can.'

'If you don't mind my asking, where do you see

your situation going?'

'No, I don't mind, but to tell you the truth I don't know. Like you, I've fallen for an American, and I want to spend my life with him ... but there's Adam.' She let out a deep sigh. 'I'm just living for each day at the moment.'

'Life's a bitch, isn't it?'

Jenny burst out laughing. 'I couldn't have put it better myself. Look, why don't you come over to my place for lunch on Sunday?' Seeing Rusty's worried expression she added, 'I'll be all on my own, and I'll be glad of the company, honestly. Please say you'll come.'

And Rusty agreed to do so.

But when Jenny arrived home and opened her mail, she realized that she now had a big problem. Adam was coming home. He'd been injured, not seriously, but he'd caught some shrapnel in his leg and had been flown home after an operation, to recover. He would be arriving on Monday.

She sat at the table in the kitchen and looked out of the window. She was sorry he'd been injured – of course she was – but the idea of having him here, wanting her to be at his beck and call, filled her with trepidation. The idea of sharing a bed with him made her go cold. She didn't want him to touch her, and when he was well enough she couldn't bear the idea of his making love to her. She knew she just couldn't do it. She closed her eyes, but the thoughts of the difficulties ahead would not go away. What on earth was she to do? She picked up the phone and called Chad.

Young Sarah was also suffering, but her pain was the birth of her baby. She was in her bedroom at Cherry Tree Farm, with the midwife and Ethel Brown, who was sponging the perspiration off her forehead.

'It won't be long now, my dear, and then this will all be over. You'll forget all about the pain when you hold the baby in your arms, I promise.'

Another contraction grabbed Sarah, and she let out a cry of pain. 'You'd better be right,' she said, 'because there will only be one child! I can't do this again.'

Ethel smiled to herself, remembering having similar thoughts herself, but when half an hour later Sarah was gazing lovingly at the baby boy in her arms, she knew the girl *would* forget, as she and many other mothers had.

Sarah studied the small face of her son and was amazed. So this was what she and Gunter had made. She thought the child looked a miniature of his father and wished with all her heart he could be here to see this miracle for himself. At least she could have a picture taken and send it to Gunter. She asked Ethel to pass her hairbrush to make herself look less frazzled from the birth, and then asked her to take a picture of them, to send to the father.

'He'll be so proud of you both,' said Ethel as she aimed the lens at the bed and its occupants.

'But when ever will he see little Hans?' They had both chosen names for their baby through letters.

'Don't start finding difficulties,' warned Ethel. 'You've both come through the birth, and you

151

have a healthy child. You just tell yourself that sometime in the future you'll all be together, and that's what counts!'

At that moment there was a knock on the door, and Mr Brown asked if he could see the new arrival. He was ushered in.

He smiled at Sarah. 'Well done, girlie.' Then he leaned over the baby. 'Now, there is a handsome child if ever I saw one. Have you got a name for the little fellow?'

'Hans. Gunter and I chose it.'

'Yes, and it suits him,' he said. 'I'll leave you in peace now. But congratulations.'

That evening, Jenny opened the door to her lover and flew into his arms, in tears. 'Oh Chad, what am I going to do?' she cried.

He held her close and said, 'Hey, now, come on honey, calm down and we'll sort this out.' He led her into the drawing room and they sat on the settee. 'Now tell me what was in the letter.'

Jenny gave it to him to read.

He put down the letter and took her hand in his. 'Well, darlin', the time has come to decide the future – are we going to stay together … or not?'

She looked into his eyes and caressed the face of the man she was in love with. 'I can't live with Adam,' she said. 'I can't go back to my old life. I just can't!'

'Before you decide, you must face up to reality, Jenny honey. Can you put this comfortable life behind you? Because I'm not sure what I can offer you. I have enough money put aside to open a small ranch back home, but it will be real hard to begin with. There won't be any luxuries, not for a while, until I get established.'

'I don't care about that! I just want to spend the rest of my life with you, that's *all* I care about.'

But he was insistent. 'That's great, and you know that I want you with me, but life will be so very different. I'm just a cowboy from Wyoming, after all. I don't have the education or position that you have and are used to.'

'Do you think that matters a jot to me? You are so much more than just a cowboy; you have a gift that is amazing. I can't wait to see you use it again. I want to be part of your life, don't you believe me?'

He kissed her softly. 'Yes, I do, and I can't quite believe my luck, but what are you going to do when your husband comes home? You'll have to tell him. Are you prepared for that?'

Shaking her head she said, 'No, but it has to be done. I'll feel dreadful and Adam will be furious, but I can't lie to him, pretend that things are fine, because that wouldn't be right.'

'It may mean you'll lose everything,' said Chad. 'Your home, your friends ... and we'll have to wait until the war is over before we can be together. It could be some time. I'm asking a lot from you, Jenny. Are you really sure? Don't you want time to think this thing through?'

She smiled fondly at him. 'I can't wait to see your world; it sounds so different. Sitting round a campfire, tending to the land, looking after the horses. Don't you see, Chad, to me it sounds like heaven.'

He laughed. 'That's your free spirit emerging; I told you a long way back you would eventually understand. The real you will blossom once we get to Wyoming, and I can't wait to see that woman.'

And as she lay in his arms that night, Jenny could hardly wait to start her new life, but she knew that before that happened she would have a very rocky ride. She had no idea how Adam would react to her news. *Would* she be ostracized by all their friends? So what if she was! She could put up with that; after all, she was a woman with a mind of her own, and she'd made a decision – and as far as the others were concerned, they could like it or lump it! Chad would no longer be her guilty pleasure; she would be able to meet him openly once she'd spoken to Adam.

She looked at the face of the man sleeping beside her and knew she'd made the right decision. Come what may.

Sixteen

When Rusty arrived at Jenny's house on the Sunday, she could see that there was something on Jenny's mind, and after making some coffee, Jenny explained her situation.

After listening carefully Rusty said, 'Well, at least you know you have a future with Chad, but I don't envy you having to tell Adam. Oh, Jenny, war is hell! It messes up so many lives. Without it

we would both be going our own way as usual –
without complications.'

With a rueful smile, Jenny said, 'I don't know
about that! Living with Adam was always complicated, and I'm sure your life had its moments
too.'

Rusty chuckled softly. 'Oh yes, a few, I have to
admit. But how will Adam take it, do you think?'

Pondering on this, Jenny said, 'I'm really not
sure. When he was home last time he said I'd
changed, that he didn't know me any more – and
he was right, of course. I'd carved out a life for
myself; I was at last my own person. Mind you, at
that time I'd only seen Chad at the stables, we
hadn't become lovers yet.'

'Will you still be able to stay here?'

'I've no idea. Adam is only home until he re-
covers from the operation. It's not the best time
to be told his wife is in love with another man.
But I don't have a choice.'

'Well, if you have to leave, I have a spare bedroom going at my flat. You're very welcome to
move in with me.'

'Oh, Rusty, that's so good of you. I may have to
take up your invitation for a while until I can sort
myself out. Thank you. Anyway, let's put all this
behind us. Whilst the lunch is cooking come and
walk around the garden, it's looking lovely at the
moment.'

They sat on the garden bench after and gazed
around. 'Wyoming will be a very different land-
scape to this,' Jenny remarked quietly. 'America is
so vast in comparison.'

'You'll find it strange to begin with, I'm sure,'

Rusty agreed.

'Yes, but so exciting! I can hardly wait, but of course I'll have to.'

'That will be the hardest part. Then, when the war is over, the GIs will go home to be repatriated.' She looked at her hostess. 'I do hope you don't have to wait too long.'

Jenny put her hand over Rusty's. 'I only wish that you and Brad could make it up between you. You belong together.'

'Sadly, there is no hope of that. It's a shame because, like you with Chad, I would have followed him anywhere, without a backward glance.'

At the end of the day, as she was leaving, Rusty gave Jenny her address. 'You know where I work if you need to get in touch with me during the day.' She hugged her. 'I do hope when Adam comes home tomorrow that things won't be too difficult. Please let me know what happens, I'll be worrying about you, but remember you have a place to stay if you need it.'

As she watched Rusty walk down the path, Jenny thought: *What a marvellous girl.* If only she could talk to Brad and make him see sense. There were two people who were about to leave their life in ruins ... for what? Rusty wasn't a bad woman; if only Brad could accept her past, they could be happy together. But as she closed the door, she knew that tomorrow she was going to have to face her husband, and she felt nauseous at the thought of what lay before her.

Adam Procter sat in the military ambulance as it took him out of the town towards Chilworth. His leg was sore from the operation, and after several sleepless nights, he was somewhat irritable. How good it would be to be home, in his own house with Jenny to care for him. The doctors had done a good job, apparently, and when he was recovered he would be recalled to duty.

He was able to walk with the aid of a stick and needed to exercise his leg – walking round the garden would do that to begin with. It should take about a month for the wound to heal, he'd been told. His own doctor had been informed and would be visiting him tomorrow to change the dressing.

As the vehicle turned into his driveway, he wondered how Jenny was. He hoped she'd no longer be involved with so many committees, as he needed her to care for him. She'd have to find the time for him whilst he was home, no matter what else she had to do.

Jenny waited at the front door as the ambulance drew up beside her. The driver got out and smiled at her as he walked around to the back of the vehicle and helped the patient down.

Adam looked better than she expected, she thought thankfully, and he seemed to be walking reasonably well. She went up to him and kissed him briefly on the cheek. 'How are you?' she asked.

'Weary, and a bit stiff.' He turned to thank the driver and then entered the house.

'Would you like a cup of tea?' she asked.

'No thanks, I want something a bit stronger. A large gin and tonic would be nice.'

'Are you allowed alcohol? I wondered if you

were on any medication,' she added hastily when she saw the look of irritation on his face.

'I've finished all the antibiotics, so it's all right.' He lowered himself on to the settee. 'It's good to be home. They needed the bed so were quite happy to let me go. Dr Bailey is calling tomorrow to give me the once over,' he said as he took the glass from her. 'Aren't you having one?'

'No, it's a bit early for me. I have a coffee in the kitchen. I'll just go and get it.'

Once in the kitchen, Jenny took a deep breath. This wasn't going to be easy. She'd have to wait for the right moment to talk to him about Chad; she couldn't blurt it all out the minute he arrived. She picked up her cup and returned to the sitting room and sat in an armchair opposite her husband. 'How long do you think you'll be home?'

'They said about a month. It was quite a nasty wound, but they managed to get the pieces of shrapnel out eventually, and they grafted a bit of skin they took from my thigh to cover the gash in my leg.'

'I am sorry, that must have been very painful.'

'It wasn't a barrel of laughs, and at one stage it became infected – but at least I'm alive, unlike some poor devils.' He glanced through the window. 'The garden looks nice.'

'Well, the roses need deadheading, but the shrubs are fine.'

'And what have you been up to whilst I've been away?' He didn't give her chance to answer. 'I do hope you aren't as tied up as last time I was home because you'll need to look after me.'

Already his dictatorial tone was getting on her

nerves, and Jenny wondered just how long she'd be able to tolerate it... But the man was wounded, she'd have to remember that and try to be patient.

'Well, I *am* still busy,' she told him, 'and we'll have to come to some arrangement when I know just exactly how much nursing you'll be needing. At least you can get about, which is great.'

'I wouldn't want to get in the way of your work,' he said with heavy sarcasm.

'Don't start, Adam! You've been in the house less than half an hour. Let us at least try to understand one another.'

'I forget you're used to living alone these days, and my return must seem like an intrusion, but do remember I've been fighting in the bloody war! You could take that into consideration.'

She didn't retaliate; what was the point? 'Are you hungry?' she asked. 'Only, I've got a shepherd's pie in the oven and there are a load of fresh vegetables from the garden. You'll feel better with a good meal inside you.'

'Yes, now you come to mention it, I'm ravenous. I didn't sleep well last night, so if you don't mind I'll go to our room after and take a nap.'

Lunch wasn't too difficult. Adam told her about the fighting he'd been involved with and how he was in one way pleased to be sent to a military hospital as he could get a bit of peace and a rest.

'We're all so tired,' he explained. 'At times you just grab a sleep when and where you can. I can't wait to put my head down in my own bed.' But when he eventually went upstairs and into their bedroom – with Jenny behind him, carrying his

159

suitcase – he stopped short and frowned. 'What's this? There is only one set of pillows on my side.'

'I've moved into one of the spare rooms,' she said. 'I thought you'd sleep better on your own, and I'd be worried all the time that I might inadvertently knock your wound as I turned over.'

'Very thoughtful of you, and for a while that's probably wise. You can move back in when it's healed.'

She didn't answer.

Downstairs in the quiet of the kitchen, she sat and drank a fresh cup of coffee, thankful that Adam was now asleep. Of course she wouldn't be moving back into their bedroom, and by the time that Adam was that well recovered, she would have given him her news. She decided it was only fair to give him time to recover first. He had been through so much; it would be cruel in the extreme to tell him before he was on the road to recovery. Chad would surely understand that.

At headquarters, Chad kept glancing at his watch, wondering if Adam Procter had arrived home, and if he had, how things were going. He wanted to pick up the phone and call Jenny, but realized how unwise that would be at this moment. Jenny had said she would call the office when she could, and he'd have to be content to wait. But he was restless.

At lunchtime he couldn't face the canteen and walked to the edge of the camp, found a quiet spot and sat on the grass. He couldn't help but worry about the life that Jenny was giving up to be with him. Not her marriage. He'd been aware that was in trouble when first they met; otherwise, when he'd realized he was in love with her, he simply wouldn't have told her. She was such a classy woman, and the life they would share would be so simple in comparison. But deep down he knew she'd thrive on it. The difference in their ages had long ceased to be a problem. In fact, it had never been so with him. It had worried Jenny to begin with, he thought, but thankfully, not any longer.

He could picture them riding the range together, rounding up horses, sitting beneath the stars when they sometimes camped out. But before that could happen, there was many a fence to be jumped; not least Jenny having to tell her husband she was leaving him. Chad had suggested that he be with her when she did so, but Jenny had been adamant. She had to do it alone.

He got up and returned to his office.

The next few days were a nightmare for Jenny. The doctor had called and changed Adam's dressing. She glanced at the wound, which still looked quite nasty, and afterwards Adam had been his usual demanding self and she'd hardly had a moment to breathe. But today she'd driven him to his golf club, where he was going to meet old friends and stay for lunch. She delivered him safely and drove to the stables where Chad was waiting for her. She had managed to call him when she knew she'd be free.

As she drove into the yard, he was waiting for her. She parked the car and ran into his arms. 'Just hold me,' she cried. 'I need to feel safe.'

Chad could feel her trembling, and he tilted her chin upwards and kissed her. 'Calm down, honey, I'm here now.' He led her to the kitchen, where Beth had told him to take her so they could have some privacy to talk.

He poured them both a cup of coffee, then sat beside her. Putting a comforting arm around her he asked, 'Is it that bad, darlin'?'

She sipped her drink. 'Well, Adam is Adam. Nothing changes. I'm not sure just how long I can keep up this pretence. I'm sleeping in the spare room. I told him he would get a better night's sleep. I can't help feeling guilty, knowing what I plan to do.'

'If you feel that bad, Jenny, then sit down and tell him, as you said you would.'

'I thought I should wait until he's stronger. After all, he's been through a lot and it's going to come as a great shock to him.'

Chad gave her a hard stare. 'You haven't changed your mind, have you?'

'Oh my God, no! Seeing him again, I know that even if you were not in my life I couldn't live with Adam as his wife, not any more.'

He was relieved. 'You had me a mite worried there for a moment.'

She laughed and kissed him. 'You are stuck with me, you crazy cowboy, like it or not!'

The next three hours was heaven for Jenny. Being with Chad had given her an inner strength, and she drove to collect Adam with a much lighter heart, which he noticed when she walked into the club to collect him, but he didn't say anything until they were in the car.

162

'Well, you look happier than I've seen you since I arrived home. Where have you been to make such a change?'

She was somewhat startled by his remark. 'I went to see Beth at the stables, that's all.' But Adam didn't look convinced.

'Is that really all?'

'I didn't have time to go anywhere else,' she said tartly. Thinking she would have to be careful to hide her happiness if she saw Chad again.

At the prisoner of war camp at Bishop's Waltham, Gunter Reinhardt sat beaming with delight as he looked at the snaps of his new son, Hans. He blinked away tears of emotion as he gazed at Sarah holding the baby. Their son, how wonderful! He silently vowed that no matter what difficulties lay before them, he would be united with his family one day and his son would have a secure future. He put the letter and picture in his pocket and walked towards the main office, where he asked permission to see the officer in charge.

When eventually he was admitted, he stood to attention and made his request. 'Today, sir, I received a letter from my fiancée with a photograph of our son, born last week.'

The officer looked surprised. 'Your fiancée?'

'Yes, sir, we met when I was held in Southampton, and we fell in love. I asked Sarah to be my wife, and she accepted.'

'How the hell did you manage to make her pregnant if you were interned?'

'I was working on a small farm for several months, and the farmer allowed her to visit, sir.'

The officer murmured his disapproval. 'So why are you here?'

Gunter removed the photograph from his pocket and showed it to the man. 'Here they are, sir,' he said proudly. 'I was wondering if there was some way they could visit me so I could see them ... just this once?' He hesitated, then added, 'I intend to take them to Germany after the war. I want to have my family with me, sir.'

The officer looked at the photograph. He had children of his own, and he'd heard the yearning in the young man's voice as he spoke. He had quickly looked at Gunter's papers when he was asked for the interview, had seen his background and the report from Farmer Brown about his work on his farm. He'd liked what he'd read. This young man was no threat to the country, just a soldier doing his job, as was he.

'Very well, Reinhardt. Seeing you have a new baby, I'll give my permission... Just this once, you understand? This is a one-off.'

Gunter beamed at him. 'Thank you, sir; I won't forget your kindness. Thank you.'

'Find out when they can come, and let me know. Dismiss!'

Gunter rushed to his room and wrote to Sarah, telling her the good news. He could hardly wait to see them both; it would help him tolerate being in captivity for the rest of the war. Now he had a family of his own, and it felt so good.

He lay on his bed and let his mind conjure pictures of the future. He would want to continue with his studies, if at all possible, and then when he'd passed all his exams, he'd open a practice or maybe join his father in his. They would have a nice house on the outskirts of Hamburg. He'd teach Sarah German. Little Hans would learn it at school, but they would speak English at home so the boy would be bilingual. And so he dreamed for the rest of the day until the camp lights were turned off. He slept with a smile, the smile of a new father.

Seventeen

Adam had been home for a week when everything came to a head. He had walked up to Jenny, put his arms around her, one hand on her breast as he nuzzled her neck – and she'd frozen!

'What's the matter?' he asked angrily as she pushed his hand away. 'I am your husband, after all.' He stepped towards her, but she put out her hand to stop him.

Taking a deep breath she said, 'Come into the sitting room, we need to talk.' She tucked her trembling hands into the pockets of her cardigan.

Adam sat on the settee and waited impatiently. 'Well, what the devil do we have to talk about?'

Jenny sat opposite him. 'I'm sorry, Adam, but I want a divorce.'

'You what?'

'I want a divorce.'

His face flushed with fury. 'I've never heard anything so ridiculous in all my life!'

'I'm in love with another man.' She thought he

was going to have a fit.

'In love...' He rose from his chair and stomped up and down, then stopped in front of her. 'So who is this *other man?*'

'He's an American soldier.'

He scowled. 'Not Captain Jackson, the man you seem to meet up with all the time.'

'No, not Captain Jackson. His name is Chad Maxwell.'

'Another bloody officer, I suppose?'

Jenny tried to remain calm. 'No, as a matter of fact he's a corporal.'

'A bloody corporal? Are you serious?'

'To me his rank is of no importance. I love him for what he is.'

'And what is he exactly?'

'He's a horse whisperer; he tames wild horses.'

'He sounds like a bloody cowboy!'

Jenny stared straight at him. 'Yes, precisely. He's going to buy a ranch in Wyoming after the war and raise horses.'

He gazed at her in disbelief. 'You mean to say you'd give up all this–' he gestured with his hand around the room – 'to live on some ranch in the middle of nowhere with some cowboy? Have you completely lost your marbles?'

'I know it sounds strange to you, Adam, as you have always liked material things, but to live a simple life with Chad, riding the range, to me sounds like heaven.'

'Chad? What kind of name is that for God's sake?'

'It really doesn't matter. I'm sorry, Adam, none of this was planned, it just happened.'

He sat back down on the settee. 'I can't believe I'm hearing this. Christ, Jenny, we've been married for years. I thought you were happy.'

'I was to begin with, but as the years passed, it became just a routine.'

'Thanks a bunch!'

'You said when you came home last time that I had changed – well, it was true. I suddenly discovered I was a person, not an appendage. I like the woman I found, but unfortunately for you, I no longer want my old life. I no longer want to be your wife. I want a divorce.'

He suddenly realized she was serious, and anger took over from disbelief. 'If that's what you want, then go to your bloody cowboy. Pack your stuff and get out!'

'But what about you, Adam? You need looking after until you're better.'

'It's a little late to be concerned about my welfare, isn't it?' he said bitterly.

'I'm quite prepared to stay and look after you until you're well enough to return to your unit.'

'That's very big of you! No thanks. Do you think I would want you around me knowing you would rather be with another man? No. I'll hire a nurse and a housekeeper. Now, I suggest you pack a bag.' He got out of the chair and limped out of the room to his study.

Jenny heard the door slam. Although she didn't regret her decision for a moment, she was sorry she'd had to break the news to Adam when he was still injured, but she'd had no choice. She couldn't bear him to touch her. Not now.

She went upstairs to her bedroom and, getting

out a large suitcase, started to pack her clothes. She would collect the rest of her things when Adam had returned to his unit. She would go to Rusty's flat for a while until she sorted herself out – she would have to rent a flat and find a job. There were sufficient funds in her bank account to see her through until then. Although she and Adam had a joint account, she had always had an account in her own name – which, as things had turned out, was just as well.

Adam stood at the study window and watched Jenny put her case in the boot of her car and drive away, using the petrol she was allowed to do her war work. He was stunned. He could hardly believe what was happening. Jenny must be completely mad, he thought. How could she give up her comfortable way of life with him to go and live in Wyoming – with a bloody cowboy, for Christ's sake! What's more, she seemed completely enamoured with this man.

He lit a cigarette. *She'll soon come to her senses,* he told himself. The war would have to end first, then time would pass before she could go to the States. But if she changed her mind, did he even want her back? All these thoughts clouded his brain until he couldn't think straight. He'd call a taxi and go to his club for a meal, a couple of drinks, and then come home. Perhaps then he could make some sense of what happened. Tomorrow he'd call an agency and hire a housekeeper and get a nurse to look after his medical needs until he was well. Maybe by then Jenny would have come to her senses and he would then decide what to do about their marriage.

Jenny and Rusty sat in the small lounge of Rusty's flat, eating baked beans on toast, washed down by a not particularly good bottle of red wine.

'I'll have to look for a job tomorrow,' Jenny said.

'Doing what?'

'I'll look in the *Echo* and see what's on offer. I'm good at administration, so maybe something to do with the military. After all, I'm already working with them.'

'Why don't you have a word with Brad?'

'Yes, I could do that I suppose. I'll wait and see what's in the paper first. By the way, I rang Chad and told him I was here and gave him this address. I hope you don't mind?'

'Look, Jenny, this is your home for as long as you want it, and you have your own key, so stop worrying ... and if you want Chad to stay overnight, that's fine too.' She chuckled softly. 'Mind you, it will be a bit of a squeeze with two of you in a single bed!'

'Thanks, Rusty, what would I do without you?'

'Don't be silly. You'd have done the same for me.' She rose to her feet. 'I'm off to bed; I have to be up for work in the morning.'

'I'll go shopping for food tomorrow. I've brought my ration book; I'll see what I can find. I'll have a meal ready for when you get home.'

'How lovely! And to have company. I've felt really lonely since I moved here.'

There was a plaintive note to her voice, and

Jenny felt sorry that the situation between her friend and Brad was so bad. She wondered if there wasn't something she could do to change this.

The following morning Jenny caught the tram and went to army headquarters and asked to speak to Captain Jackson. Chad came from the outer office, grinned broadly at her and said, 'Would you come this way, Mrs Procter?'

Brad walked round his desk, kissed her on the cheek and said, 'Chad told me about your husband. Sit down, Jenny, what can I do for you?'

She explained her situation. 'I'm looking for a job. I wondered if you knew of anything.'

'As a matter of fact, I do! We've set up a department to deal with war brides–' he smiled at her – 'which is something I know that you will be interested in personally in the future. Several of our men have met British girls and have already married them, and others plan to do so in the near future. After the war is over, we will have to ship these women out to the States, of course, but there are several steps that have to be taken before this can happen. You will have to liaise with the Red Cross – and us, of course, but you do that already so know the drill. I'll bring some papers over to your place late this afternoon if you like, and we can go over them together so you'll understand just what I want from you.'

'That's marvellous! Thank you, Brad, I'll really enjoy doing that.' She gave him her new address without telling him that she was staying with Rusty.

On the way home, Jenny joined several queues for food and eventually returned with some sausages, a rabbit and some vegetables, thinking all the while of the vegetables growing in her garden at home, which would be going to waste. She would make a good rabbit stew for this evening, which would perhaps help to cheer her friend and fill in her time waiting for Brad to call.

The American arrived late in the afternoon, laden with coffee, eggs, fruit and butter. 'I thought this would help out,' he said as he unpacked the goods.

Jenny was most grateful and even more delighted when he produced a tin of ham.

They sat down together and went through the papers he'd brought with him, discussing the finer details and what would be required of Jenny.

'I only hope these girls realize what they're letting themselves in for,' he said. 'I'm sure that many of the men have shot their women a line about their homes and lives back in the States, and some, I'm sure, are in for a big disappointment when they get there. But that's out of my hands. We've talked to the guys about doing this, of course, but that's all we can do.'

'If they really love their man, they'll put up with a lot before quitting,' Jenny said with conviction.

He smiled at her. 'I don't think you have a thing to worry about with Chad – he's a great guy.'

'I think so.' As she spoke, Jenny heard the front door being opened.

Rusty walked into the room and was shocked to

see Brad sitting there. They looked at each other in surprise.

'This is Rusty's flat,' Jenny explained. 'She offered me a room when Adam kicked me out. I'll go and make us some coffee.'

Left alone, neither Brad nor Rusty knew what to say. Brad broke the silence first. 'You're looking well. How've you been?'

'Fine, thanks.' Rusty felt her heart pounding, she wanted to reach out and touch him.

'Rusty's working at Edwin Jones,' called Jenny from the kitchen.

'Is that right?' Brad asked with surprise.

'Yes, I got the job just before the last time we met. As you can see, I've moved. I've started a new life altogether,' she said hopefully.

'That's good to hear.' Brad looked at his watch. 'I'd better be on my way.' Getting to his feet, he walked to the kitchen door 'I'll be in touch, Jenny, when I've set you up with an office. Probably by Monday. Gotta fly.' He smiled across at Rusty. 'Good to see you again.' And he left the flat.

Jenny walked back into the room. Rusty was sitting looking devastated.

'That didn't turn out quite as I had hoped,' Jenny told her as she sat beside her. 'Sorry I didn't tell you Brad was coming. I hoped once he saw you...'

Her friend grimaced and forced a smile. 'It was a nice try, Jenny, and I thank you for the thought, but as you see, it really is over as far as Brad is concerned. Oh well! Any tea in that pot?' And the subject was closed.

Eighteen

Brad Jackson drove away from Rusty's flat, his equilibrium definitely shaken. The last person he'd expected to see was the beautiful redhead with whom he'd shared so many romantic and intimate moments. How well she looked, and how shocked she was to see him there, but once that moment had passed – how tenderly she had looked at him. He pulled over to the side of the road and looked over Southampton Water. He got out of the jeep, lit a cigarette and walked over the grass and perched on a large piece of stone, staring into space.

God! How he'd missed her! His life with her around had seemed so full. Without her, it had no purpose, and now she was working at a proper job and had been, apparently, since before their last meeting. But why had she waited so long to do so? Why didn't she do so when first they met – or at least when they became lovers? He mentally argued with himself for the next fifteen minutes before getting in the car and driving back to the flat and ringing the bell with great insistence.

'All right! I'm coming!' Rusty yelled as she went to open the door.

'Get your coat, you're coming with me!' Brad demanded.

Jenny watched in amazement as Rusty grabbed

her overcoat and was hauled out of the room by Brad, who was looking more than a little determined.

Brad drove up the Avenue and parked the jeep outside the Cowherds Inn, on the edge of the common, which was now commandeered by the American forces. He stopped the jeep, turned off the engine, turned towards Rusty, took her into his arms and kissed her until neither of them could breathe.

Gasping for air, Rusty said, 'Bloody hell! Well, that was almost worth waiting so long for!'

'What do you mean ... almost?' Brad asked, slightly put out.

'What I meant was it was a long time coming! Sooner would have been better.'

'We need to talk, Rusty,' he said.

'No, Brad, we don't. All you need to ask yourself is this: can you forget I was a prostitute, or will it be for ever between us? It's as simple as that. Do you love me enough to let it go?'

He gazed at her with admiration. 'Oh, Rusty, how simple you make life sound, you see life so clearly. Is it really that easy?'

'That's up to you, Brad. I gave that life up for you – for us. Now it's up to you to decide if we have a future or not.'

He looked into the brown eyes that challenged him. Eyes that were honest, with nothing more to hide ... and were full of hope. How could he resist? Why would he even want to? He cupped her face in his hands and kissed her gently.

'I see a great future ahead of us, Rusty darling. Come on, let's celebrate! We'll see what they've got on the menu in the dining room,' and he climbed out of the car, collected her from the passenger side, and with a broad grin put his arm round her and walked towards the entrance.

Rusty was almost too afraid to breathe. Could this really be happening? Did Brad really mean what he said? When he had time to think, would he still be of the same mind? All these thoughts tumbled through her mind, but she pushed them aside as they walked into the dining room. The man she adored was with her again, she'd just take each day as it came ... but with everything crossed!

Adam Procter was not so happy. It had been several days now since Jenny had packed her bag and driven away. He had no idea where she was, and when he went to his club to seek out some company he'd had to field questions about his wife.

'She's well, thank you. Jenny's really busy at the moment; you know how involved she's become with various committees.'

So far, no one knew she'd gone or the reason behind her leaving – and he planned to keep it that way.

He'd hired a housekeeper, an older woman who didn't ask questions, and a nurse who came in twice a day to change his dressings and see he took his medicine. He was able to fend for himself, other than that. He was well able to dress himself and give himself a good wash down. When his wound was healed, then he'd be able to take a bath. But with every day that passed his bitterness grew. How could Jenny turn her back on all they had built together to run off with a bloody Yank? What sort of man was he, this cowboy who had tempted his wife so strongly that she'd turned her back on him? His curiosity grew and grew until he had to meet this man himself. He remembered that Jenny had spoken about an American doing work at the stables... What had she called him? A horse whisperer – that was it. He'd go to the stables tomorrow and see if he couldn't arrange a meeting with this fellow. Perhaps then he could settle the matter once and for all and put a stop to this ridiculous nonsense!

Chad had a day's leave and was helping Beth settle a new mare which had been brought in to the stable by its owner who was no longer able to care for it. The mare was in foal and unsettled by the change. Beth had been concerned that the mare would be stressed enough to endanger the foal she was carrying, and Chad said he would help her settle down. He was in the stable working with the animal when Adam Procter arrived, having been given a lift by a friend.

Chad heard the man talking to Beth. He could hardly miss the loud and imperious tone of the voice as the stranger asked about the horse whisperer he'd heard about. He guessed immediately the identity of the speaker and walked out of the stable, closing the door behind him.

Walking up to the man, Chad said, 'I believe it's me you're looking for. I'm Chad Maxwell, and if I'm not mistaken you are Captain Procter.'

Adam could hardly hide his surprise when he looked at the American. He was much younger than he expected; he also appeared to be very calm, considering he was facing the husband of his lover! But before he could say anything, it was Chad that spoke.

'Captain Procter, I think we need to sit down and talk, man to man.' He looked at Beth who was standing by, looking more than a little perturbed. 'May we use your kitchen?' Chad asked her.

'Of course. Help yourself to tea or coffee.' She walked away and left them together.

Once in the kitchen, Chad filled the kettle and plugged it in. 'Tea or coffee?' he asked.

'Neither, thank you! This isn't a bloody social call. I've come to talk about my wife!'

Chad calmly sat down. 'Of course you have. Right, shoot!'

Adam looked at him in astonishment. 'Is that all you have to say? You Yanks really do take the cake! You steal my wife away from a marriage of nineteen happy years and sit there and say ... shoot! This is serious stuff, not one of your Hollywood films. You are about to ruin her life, and I won't let you get away with it!'

'I can understand your anger, Captain, but I have to question you about your marriage being happy. It wasn't – at least, not for the latter years.'

'What the hell do you know about it?'

'I know that when I met your wife she was happy. After all, she was free to be her own person, do the things that really interested her – for once.'

177

'That is very presumptuous of you.'

'Not really. Your wife is a free spirit whose character had been swamped by living with you. She had completely lost her identity. Now, happily, she knows who she is and what she wants out of life. Fortunately for me, she wants to come to Wyoming.'

'What rubbish! Jenny has no idea what she wants.'

'Have you ever asked her?'

Adam became flustered. 'Of course not, she's my wife; I know what's best for her.'

Chad raised his eyebrows in surprise, then frowned. 'There you have the crux of your problem, Captain Procter. Her needs are secondary to your own. You have no idea what sort of woman you married.'

'Of course I do! Good God, man! I have been married to her long enough.'

'Then tell me this. What's her favourite flower?'

Adam didn't hesitate. 'She's a gardener, so she loves all sorts of flowers.'

'Wrong! The poppy is her favourite. What's her ambition?'

Here the man was completely flummoxed.

'You didn't know she had one did you? She wants to ride out with her favourite horse and camp beneath the stars.'

'Jenny would hate that! She likes her creature comforts.'

Chad just shook his head. 'I feel so sorry for you, sir. You have been married to the most wonderful woman for nineteen years, and yet you don't know or understand her – and what's more, you have never even tried. That takes tremendous arrogance. You don't deserve such a woman!'

'And you do?'

'Probably not, if I'm honest. I didn't plan to fall in love with Jenny or she with me, it just happened, but let me tell you, I feel the luckiest guy on this planet. Believe me, I won't waste a moment of the time that we are together, no siree!'

Adam looked at Chad with contempt. 'You really think she's coming to live with you, don't you? Well, let me put you in the picture, my young friend; Jenny has just been carried away by the moment, as so many other women in wartime have. I was away, and you, a younger man, paid her some attention, which was flattering to an older woman. She loves her home, her garden – being my wife. As soon as you go away, she'll come to her senses. This, this ... thing with you will pass in time, and we will get over it and move on.'

'That's up to Jenny. I give you my word that I won't push her either way. It will be totally up to her, but I have to warn you, Captain Procter, you will be the loser, because I know what makes Jenny tick, and sadly, you have no idea!' He rose from the chair. 'Forgive me, but I have an unhappy mare to see to.'

Adam glared at the American. 'I suppose you think you can understand the human spirit as well as you can understand a sick animal?'

'I'm amazed that you even recognize the fact of a human spirit. Maybe there's hope for you yet, Captain, but sadly not with your own wife! You left that far too late!'

Adam sat in the kitchen chair, fuming. How dare this whippersnapper tell him he didn't understand his own wife! Well, one thing he was certain of was this young man was definitely not Jenny's type at all! That much he did know. Let her have her moment of madness. He'd shortly be back with his company, but the American must soon be sent to Europe; when eventually the war was over, time would sort them out. She'd be happy to come home. He could wait.

Beth saw Adam Procter leave the stable and wait at the gate to be picked up. She wandered over to the stable and seeing Chad asked, 'Everything all right?'

He shrugged. 'As far as I'm concerned, but I don't think the Captain would agree.' He smiled at her. 'Don't worry, Beth, no blood was drawn!'

She chuckled and walked away, thinking that no two men could be more different than Jenny's husband and her lover. She had no doubt about which man she preferred.

An hour later, Jenny arrived at the stables to help out. She soon found Chad and watched him work with the mare, who by now seemed more settled. She saw Chad feel the swollen stomach of the animal, talking softly as he did so. Then, with a final pat and stroke of the animal's mane, he left the stable. Seeing Jenny waiting, he took her into his arms and kissed her.

'How's my girl?'

'Fine, and how are you?'

'I'm real good. I had a visit from your husband today; we sat and chatted.'

Jenny looked shattered. 'Oh my God!'

'It's OK, honey, we sat and talked in a civilized manner.'

She didn't know what to say for a moment. 'And what happened?'

'The captain told me that in time you would go back to him. He inferred this was just a moment of madness on your part and you would get over it.'

'Do you believe that, Chad?'

'Not for one moment, but he does. Poor man, he doesn't know you at all after all these years, and that's partly your fault, Jenny.'

'Whatever do you mean?'

'You let him take you over without a fight. You should have stood your ground, been the person that I know you are deep down. You let him swamp you with his own personality.'

She gave a wry smile. 'But when we were first married he was very much my hero. He was determined, sure of himself, I admired him immensely.'

'And now, all these years later?'

'I suppose, anything for a quiet life. You get into a routine and just go with the flow. My God, that sounds so weak, doesn't it?'

'You said it honey, not me.'

'Then when he went away, I was free to do the things I wanted ... and then of course I met you.' She gazed fondly at him. 'Then I wanted even more.'

Pulling her into his arms, Chad kissed her softly. 'I've finished here. I still have until late tonight and I want to make love to you, so why don't we go back to the flat and there we can be alone?' He held her even closer until she could feel his arousal. His hand gently caressed her backside, and she couldn't concentrate.

'Let's go,' she managed to whisper. And they left the stables.

Nineteen

Gunter Reinhardt was beside himself with excitement. Today he was to see his son for the very first time and Sarah, the mother of his baby and the woman he intended to marry, come what may!

Ethel Brown the farmer's wife was to accompany Sarah and baby Hans on the train, which was a great relief to him. The kindness of strangers, thought Gunter as he waited. After all, the Browns hardly knew him apart from the time he'd worked for them, but they had taken Sarah into their home when her own family had disowned her. How could he ever repay such kindness?

He was ushered into a small common room by one of the British soldiers on duty and told to wait. He tried to sit patiently, but before long he was pacing the small room until he heard the door open and there stood Sarah with a small bundle in her arms. She stood, smiling at him, with tears streaming down her face.

He stepped forward. *'Liebling!'* He carefully took her and her baby into his arms, kissing her first and then looking down at his firstborn. '*Mein Gott!* Is this really our son?'

'Yes, Gunter darling, this is Hans.' She handed the baby over to him. 'I think he looks a lot like you.'

He gazed at the baby, taking in every small detail. He gently held the baby's hand and was overcome when the tiny fingers closed around one of his. He looked up at Sarah with tears brimming his eyes. 'Did you see that?' He carefully placed the baby on his shoulder, breathing in the scent of him. 'He's wonderful. And how are you, my *liebling?*'

'I'm fine. The Browns are wonderful to us both. I help Ethel in the house; we get along very well.' Her voice broke. 'Oh Gunter, I thought I'd never see you again.'

He caught hold of her hand. 'We are a family, Sarah. No one will ever come between us. No matter what, or how long it takes, we will be together after the war, I promise!' The baby gurgled. 'There! You see, little Hans totally agrees with me.'

Gunter looked up as one of the soldiers on guard came in with a tray of tea. 'I thought your wife might need this after her long journey.'

Sarah smiled at the soldier. 'Thank you, that's so kind of you.'

The man shrugged. 'I have a baby myself, haven't seen him for several months.' He smiled and nodded at Gunter, then left them alone.

'What a nice gesture,' Sarah remarked. 'They obviously treat you well here.'

Gunter just nodded. He didn't tell her about the few sentries who treated the prisoners like dirt, who told them the only good German was a dead one. Of the insults he himself had suffered when it was known he had a child by an English girl – from his own kind, as well as from the guards. It was only a small nucleus of the men guarding them who treated them badly, but enough to make living there unpleasant.

The afternoon passed all too soon, and Sarah was told her time was up. With a voice choked with emotion she asked, 'When will I see you again?'

'I have no idea. This visit, I'm afraid, will not be repeated. I was fortunate to be allowed to see you and the baby at all. Never mind, *liebling*, we will write all the time, and one day we'll put all this behind us. You must be strong for our son.' He stood and held them both in his arms, kissing first the baby, then Sarah. 'Remember that I love you both, more than life itself.'

Sarah, too full of emotion for words, left the room to join Ethel Brown and journey home.

Gunter walked back to his room in a daze. There was joy after seeing his child and Sarah, but such sadness as he faced the fact that he might not see them again until the child was no longer a baby. He would miss seeing his son progress so much, but at least he had today. No one could take that away from him.

One of the other German prisoners put his head round the door. Seeing Gunter standing there, lost in thought, the man stepped inside. 'I hear you saw your bastard child today.'

Gunter hit him, sending him reeling into the corridor. He then shut the door.

Adam Procter had only another week left before he returned to his regiment. He had phoned Beth at the stables to ask for Jenny's address, as he had to see her to make arrangements before he left. Beth wouldn't give the address to him without Jenny's permission, but she said she would pass on the message, which she did – and Jenny had called her husband and arranged to go to the house to see him.

As she drove up the drive, she looked at her garden with a certain longing. She loved working in it when she'd been living there, and although it was tidy to a point, it was obvious to her that it needed someone who really cared about it. She drew up in front of the house, got out of the car and walked to the door. Here she paused; she had her own key, but it didn't seem right to just walk in, so she rang the bell.

Adam opened the door. He looked better than she expected, and she was pleased. She had felt guilty leaving him when she did, but it had been his choice to get someone else in to look after his needs.

'Hello, Adam. You're looking well,' she said.

'Yes, well, no one is indispensable,' was his terse reply, and she knew that this meeting was going to be difficult.

They went into the sitting room. Adam went to the table in the window where the drinks were kept. 'Can I get you something?' he asked.

'Not for me, thanks.' She watched as he poured himself a large gin and tonic and guessed it wasn't the first one that day – and she waited.

'I'm due to join my regiment next week, so I thought we ought to discuss a few things.'

'Like what?'

'Financial arrangements – after all, I *am* still your husband, and I must provide for you financially – and then there's the house.'

'What about the house?'

'I certainly don't want it left empty when I'm away. I don't want to sell it, and I certainly wouldn't dream of letting it to strangers.'

'So what are you suggesting?'

'That you move back in when I'm gone. It's been your home for many years, and I'm sure you wouldn't like to see it empty and neglected.'

'No, of course not!'

Adam was delighted. He hoped that once again residing in her home and seeing to the garden, which was her pride and joy, might eventually persuade Jenny that she had made a terrible mistake, wanting to leave.

'Good, I'm pleased you agree. It will also put a stop to any rumours that we've parted. I've certainly not told anyone, and I would appreciate it if you were discreet. I do *not* want to be the centre of local gossip. I will, of course, make a monthly payment into your account.'

'There's no need. I'm working and earning a living.'

He looked at her coldly. '*You* may have forgotten that you are a married woman and have a duty to me; however, I am different. As long as you are married to me, I will take care of you!'

She suddenly felt sorry for him. Adam lived his life by the rules. Rules were to be followed at all times, and now she had broken them and he didn't know how to cope.

'Thank you, Adam. Under the circumstances, I think you are being very noble.'

'The circumstances are not of my making, Jenny.' He dropped his guard for a moment. 'Can't you see what a terrible mistake you're making, how much you are throwing away? I beg you, think again before you ruin your life ... and mine!'

'I am sorry, Adam, I really am. I have thought long and hard about what I'm doing, but I haven't changed my mind, and I don't want you to go away with any false hopes. After the war, I'm going to the States to start a new life. None of this was planned, it just happened, and I cannot let the opportunity pass. I'll always regret it if I do.'

His jaw tightened. 'If you continue down this road and it doesn't work, don't think you can come crawling back to me!'

She smiled softly. 'It will work, I am certain of that. Chad and I love each other.'

'We loved each other once!' His cry of anguish touched her deeply, but there was nothing she could do to alleviate his unhappiness.

'Yes, we did, and I will always remember those early days, but we all change. You will always have a special place in my heart.'

'Don't patronize me, Jenny! If you continue with this divorce nonsense, I'll have no choice but to sue on grounds of adultery. Is that what you want ... your dirty laundry spread all over the papers?'

'It's not ideal, but I don't have any choice.'

'Yes, you do! For God's sake woman, when are you going to come to your senses?'

She stood up. 'Look, Adam, this isn't getting us anywhere. I will come back and take care of the house until you return from the war, as you wish, and after that we will go our different ways. Just take care when you're over there, wherever that is. Here is my office number if you want to contact me during the day.' She handed him a card. 'Look after yourself,' she said and picking up her handbag she left.

Later that afternoon, Jenny was surprised when Brad knocked on her office door, then entered. They hadn't a meeting planned, and she wondered why he was there. 'Something wrong?' she asked.

He sat down. 'Not in the way that you mean, Jenny, but I do have some news.'

She frowned at the seriousness of his tone. 'I have a feeling I'm not going to like what you have to say.'

'I'm being shipped out, and Chad is coming with me.'

Jenny felt a chill creep up her spine as if she was sitting in a draught. It was the news she'd been dreading. 'Oh Brad, I am so sorry. When do you leave?'

'Next week. Obviously I can't tell you more, but it's a big operation. If it's a success it could bring an end to the war. That's a big if!'

'That would be wonderful! Have you told Rusty yet?'

'I haven't had the chance, and it's Rusty I want

188

to talk to you about. You'll be alone once Chad and I have left. I just want to know you'll look after each other.'

She cast a critical glance at him. 'I do hope that you're not inferring that Rusty might go off the rails once you've left? Because if you are, I would be bitterly disappointed in you, Brad!'

'No, no, I don't mean that at all, but you'll be lonely and worried, you'll need one another for support.'

'I saw Adam earlier today, and he wants me to move back into the house when he goes to make sure it's kept up together. I had planned to ask Rusty to move in with me.'

'That would be great, Jenny. I'm sure she'd love it there.'

'Well, it's big enough, as you know, and she can help me with the garden – and as you say, we'll need one another. You just make sure my man comes back safely ... and you too, of course!'

He rose from his seat. 'Both Chad and I have an overnight pass from tonight, so I guess I'll see you later.'

When she was alone, Jenny fought back her tears. Thousands of women had been through this sort of hell, that's what war did to people. She and Rusty would just have to get on with life, but she was so grateful to have her as a friend, especially at this time.

When Chad rang her a little later they decided to meet for a meal first to give Rusty and Brad some privacy as these final days together were so special. He rang again later with a change of plans.

'Pack an overnight bag, Jenny. I've booked us a room for the night; that way we can be totally alone. We have a lot to talk about before I leave, and I don't want any interruptions. Besides, I want to hold you, make love to you, without worrying about Rusty and Brad being in the next room. I'll pick you up at seven.'

Hearing his voice made the situation all the more poignant, and she couldn't wait to see him. He had become such a part of her everyday life, and Jenny knew that when Chad eventually left there would be an enormous void, as this extraordinary man had come to mean absolutely everything to her.

She longed to experience his world. The simplicity of it sounded wonderful, and the thought of living on a ranch, of riding in wonderful surroundings, was so exciting and so different to everything she was used to. Her one worry was that she would disappoint Chad. How awful it would be if she didn't live up to his expectations. Being lovers here and now in wartime was one thing. It had a certain edge to it, an excitement. But being settled in a home, being part of normal everyday life, was very different. Well, it would be a long time before that happened, anyway. Tonight might be the last time they would be together for a very long time, and she was going to make the most of every moment.

Twenty

Jenny arrived at Rusty's flat before Brad, so it was she who broke the bad news to the redhead, and it was she who comforted her when the tears began.

'Come on, Rusty, you don't want Brad to see you all red eyed and sad. These are the last few days you'll spend together for a while, so send him away with happy memories.'

Rusty looked at her with amazement. 'How can you be so calm?'

With a wry laugh, Jenny confessed: 'Don't you fret, I shed a bucketload of tears when Brad left my office, but I've had time to recover. Now I suggest you go and have a bath, wash your hair, put on your make-up and enjoy every moment you can; I intend to. Chad has booked us in to a hotel for the night, so you'll have your captain all to yourself.'

Rusty quickly wiped away her tears. 'You're right, of course.' She giggled mischievously. 'I'll give him the time of his life!'

'Before you go, there is an offer I'd like to make to you.' Jenny explained about her visit with Adam. 'So how would you like to move in with me? It would save rent on this place, and we'd have more room.'

'Oh my God, are you really asking me to live in that beautiful house?' Her eyes were bright with excitement.

'Absolutely, or I'd be rattling around on my own. Mind you, you'd have to help me with the garden.'

Rusty hugged her. 'How marvellous! We can keep each other's spirits up.' She went to say something else, but Jenny stopped her.

'We haven't time now. I'll take the bathroom first, we need to get ready.'

Chad was the first to arrive. He whistled when he saw the girls. 'My oh my, you two look good enough to eat! Are you ready, honey? Have you packed your overnight stuff?'

Jenny told him she had, and they left the flat. They drove to a restaurant in town where Chad had booked a table, neither of them saying a word about his leaving until they'd ordered and the wine had been poured.

Chad lifted his glass. 'To us, darlin', and to our long and happy future together.'

Jenny clinked hers with his. 'To us and our future.' She sipped her drink. 'I don't know how I'm going to manage when you leave.'

'You'll do just the same as all the women in your situation; you take it a day at a time, and write ... often. But I just wanted to discuss with you my plans for after the war, so you'll know what you're letting yourself in for.'

Jenny held up her finger and hushed his flow of words. 'I don't need to know. I'll come to you wherever, whenever – the rest is just background.'

He smiled, gazed at her and shook his head in disbelief. 'You really do mean that, don't you?'

'Absolutely!'

'I don't deserve you, Jenny honey, but I promise you, you'll never ever regret what you are doing, what you are giving up for me. On that, you have my solemn oath.'

They talked about a million things during their meal. Jenny explained that she and Rusty were moving back into her house and the reason why.

'It makes good sense,' Chad agreed. 'It's a beautiful place, and I can understand why Adam wants you to look after it. It's the least you can do for him.'

They chatted about a million things until it was time to retire, and they drove to the hotel, where Chad signed the register as Mr and Mrs Maxwell, picked up the key and headed for the lift. When he found their room number, he swept Jenny up into his arms and carried her into the bedroom.

'Here we are, Mrs Maxwell, this is our trial honeymoon!' he said as he put her down.

'What do you mean, trial?'

'Well, if you don't cut the mustard and please me, I'll find me a nice little Mademoiselle to take your place!'

'You cheeky devil! I haven't heard you complain up till now!'

He pulled her close and kissed her softly. 'That's for sure. What's to complain about? You are everything I've ever wanted in a woman – and more.'

Brad arrived at the flat that evening, carrying a huge bouquet of crème roses and an extravagant box of chocolates.

193

'Good heavens, how on earth did you come by these?' Rusty asked as he handed them over.

He grinned broadly. 'I'm liable to be court-martialled. These were sent over from the States for the Colonel, but unfortunately they got lost in transit!'

She couldn't help but laugh. 'Oh Brad, thank you so much, you have no idea what a treat that is. Come in, I've made some coffee. What do you want to do this evening?'

He raised his eyebrows quizzically.

'Apart from that!' she scolded.

'As Chad and Jenny are elsewhere, I thought we'd stay in. I had one of the chefs make up a picnic for us.' He went over to the front door, opened it and brought in a box and a bottle of champagne. 'Tonight we'll celebrate.'

'I don't want to celebrate you leaving, Brad.'

'No, Rusty darling, we are going to celebrate my return – and our future.'

She put her arms around his neck. 'Are you absolutely sure that's what you want?'

'Definitely. Now put this bottle into the fridge, and let's see what the chef has done.'

They sat down to a sumptuous meal which, in the wartime conditions that prevailed, Rusty really appreciated. There was pâté to start with, followed by large prawns in a delicious sauce, a Waldorf salad, potato salad and something Brad called coleslaw – a mixture of carrot and white cabbage in mayonnaise that was really tasty. Freshly-baked bread rolls with real butter were carefully wrapped, and to finish there was a lemon cheesecake.

Rusty tucked in with great relish. 'My goodness, Brad, if the food in the States is like this, I'll pile on the pounds!'

'No, you won't, you'll soon get used to it. Anyway, you forget I'm a doctor. I'll keep an eye on you!'

As they ate, Brad told her all about Denver where they would live, about his parents, and how they would be able to spend their spare time together ... and the children he hoped they would have.

This startled Rusty. With the life she'd been leading, children were the last thing she'd thought about; her one concern had been making sure that she didn't become pregnant. Her surprise must have shown on her face because he questioned her about it.

'Don't you want a family, Rusty?'

'To be honest I hadn't thought about it. You forget, Brad, I haven't been in a serious relationship for a very long time.' Then she stopped. Why the hell had she said that? It only brought up her past.

'But now you are. I've always envisaged my household filled with children when I eventually married, that's all.'

She realized that this was a serious issue with him. 'I'm twenty-eight; you don't think that's too late?'

He roared with laughter. 'Good God, Rusty, I've delivered babies whose mothers have been well into their thirties, and a few even in their early forties.' At her shocked expression he explained: 'This was usually at the beginning of the menopause and mostly unexpected, I have to say.' He held her gaze. 'Don't you want us to have children?'

She took hold of his hand. 'I would love to have your babies – but not too many!'

'I think six is a nice round figure.'

'What?' She looked horrified.

He started laughing again. 'I'm only joking, but at least two; I was an only child and often wished I had a sibling.'

'Me too. All right, two.'

'In which case, I think I need a bit of practice. Let's leave the dishes, this is far more important.' And he led her into the bedroom.

They didn't turn on the light, but kept the curtains open, letting the moonlight from the clear sky above shed its soft glow. 'Come here,' he said, taking her into his arms. His kisses, at first soft and gentle, intensified as he caressed her body and slowly removed her clothing. Then, when they were both naked, they lay on the bed together.

'I'm really going to miss you, darling,' he murmured as his mouth moved down her body, kissing the soft mounds of her breasts. As he parted her legs, she tensed with pleasure and anticipation.

Brad's love-making was slow and sensuous, until she cried out for him to take her.

After, they lay sated and satisfied. Rusty let out a deep sigh. 'I really needed that,' she said softly.

He nuzzled her neck. 'I know just what you mean.'

They lay together, talking softly, until they fell

asleep, entwined in each other's arms.

The following morning, Rusty awoke to the smell of bacon frying, and pulling on a dressing gown she wandered into the kitchen to see Brad standing at the stove. She stood behind him and put her arms around his waist. 'That smells amazing.'

'I brought some bacon with me; as you can see, I'm always prepared. Will you make some toast whilst I cook some eggs?'

'Eggs too! My, you know the way to a woman's heart.'

'There, and here was me thinking it was my good looks and bedroom technique!'

'Oh, that too,' she told him.

They sat eating their breakfast until he had to leave. 'I may not have a chance to see you again before we ship out,' he told her as he left. Holding her close, he said, 'You take care, you hear?'

Rusty sat finishing her coffee, looking out of the window, wondering just how long it would be before the war would be over and when that happened, she tried to visualize her new life as Mrs Brad Jackson, but somehow the picture wouldn't form in her mind at all. She supposed it was because it still seemed unreal that she could have survived her life on the streets, to find such a man who knew of her past and who still wanted her. She found herself crossing her fingers as she thought about the future.

In the two weeks that followed, the men couldn't get away, but phoned the girls as often as possible. Chad managed to escape for a couple of hours and suggested to Jenny that they take a couple of mounts from the stables and have one last ride together. Knowing how much it meant to Chad to ride out into the woods, she was happy to accommodate him, calling her friend Beth to save two horses for them. She, knowing the situation, was happy to oblige, and when they arrived at the stables it was to find the horses already saddled and waiting.

'Take as long as you like,' she told them and left them alone.

Neither of them spoke as they rode out of the stable, along the country road, then turning off into the wooded area they loved so much. When they reached the middle, Chad reined in his mount, indicating to Jenny to do the same. He tied the reins to a tree, took her hand and they walked even deeper into the wood, stopping soon after. They sat on an upturned log, and he gathered her into his arms.

'Don't you just love the peaceful atmosphere of this place?' he asked her.

'Yes, it's lovely. No one could imagine sitting here that there's a war on.'

'If only that were true, honey. But we must just try and think of how great a life we'll have in Wyoming.' He looked at her with eyes shining. 'I can't wait until that day comes. We are going to have such a good time, Jenny darlin'. I long to see you blossom like a flower as you learn to enjoy the freedom you'll have living there with me.' He drew her to him and kissed her longingly. Then looking at his watch, he pursed his lips. 'We have to go, I'm afraid.'

They rode back in silence, both lost in their own thoughts.

After unsaddling the horses, Chad said good-bye to Beth and drove Jenny home. He helped her out of the jeep and held her close. 'I wish we had more time, but I have to go now. You write me as often as you can, and I'll do the same.'

She was lost for words and just clung on to him as he kissed her goodbye.

Tears streamed down her face as she watched him drive away, then she ran inside the house to her room, where she lay on the bed sobbing.

Brad had even less time to spend with Rusty, but two days before he left he was able to spend a few hours with her at the flat. They went to bed together and made love. After, they lay in each other's arms talking.

'Have you any idea at all how much longer the war will last?' asked Rusty.

'I wish I had, darling. But, honestly, it can't be that much longer.' As Brad got dressed, Rusty pulled on a dressing gown, then walked him to the door.

He held her close and ran his fingers through her hair. 'My redhead,' he whispered as he kissed her. 'Take care of yourself,' he told her. 'I'll write as often as I can, but during wartime mail delivery is uncertain, so if you don't hear for some time, don't worry. I'll be coming back for you, make no mistake!'

'You'd better, or I'll damned well come looking for you!'

He smiled at her. 'I love a woman with spirit.'

She stood at the window and watched him drive away. 'Don't you bloody well get yourself killed!' she said, then she went into the kitchen and made herself a coffee, her heart heavy, knowing it could be a very long time before they saw each other again.

Twenty-One

The following day, the two women moved into Jenny's old house. There was still a couple of weeks to go on the flat rental, but they both felt they needed to keep busy, knowing their men were due to leave these shores the following day. Neither of the women spoke of this as they moved all their belongings into the house at Chilworth.

Jenny showed Rusty to her bedroom, which was sizeable and at the back of the house, overlooking the garden.

The redhead was thrilled when she saw it. She rushed over to the window and looked out. 'Jenny, this is so beautiful, and the bedroom is so comfortable. I'll feel like a queen here.'

'I'll leave you to it,' Jenny said. 'I have to go and unpack myself.'

Adam had dismissed the housekeeper and the nurse just before he returned to his unit, so the house was clean and tidy, but in their bedroom Jenny felt saddened when she saw some of his clothes carefully draped over a chair. Poor Adam, she thought as she put them away, his world had changed, and she wondered how he would cope when eventually he came home for good, to an empty house and a wife who no longer wanted him.

She realized that she could no longer sleep in this room, the room where she'd spent so many years with him, so she moved her things into the bedroom that she and Chad had shared. There she felt more at ease. This room at least held nothing but good memories, memories that she knew would sustain her in the days and months to come. Thank God Rusty had agreed to move in with her, because she felt that she couldn't have stayed here alone.

When they'd unpacked, Jenny showed Rusty over the house, then they walked around the garden, looking at what needed doing and discussing how they would organize their day. Jenny would be able to drop Rusty at work every morning before she went to her own office, and then they could meet up to come home together.

Sitting together in the kitchen, Rusty looked around. 'You must really love Chad to give all this up,' she remarked.

Jenny dismissed her sentiment. 'This is just bricks and mortar. If I was happy with Adam, then it would be different, but with Chad, I'd happily sleep outside in the open air on a blanket, because I'd be content. Here with Adam, and the life I would have to continue to live, the house would be like a prison.' She smiled softly. 'Chad tells me I am someone special, and with him I feel as if I am. He's an extraordinary man, and I consider myself a very lucky woman.'

Rusty nodded. 'How both our lives have changed! Do you sometimes worry that you'll wake one morning to find it all a dream?'

'No, but I do wonder how long I could have gone on married to Adam. My life changed when Adam left – before I met Chad. Even without meeting him, I wanted out of my marriage, and that was a concern because I didn't know how I would manage. Now I don't have that worry. How about you?'

'My only concern is if Brad and I ever row, will he bring up my past? If he did, that could destroy us.'

'He made his decision when he came here for you, Rusty. He was an unhappy man without you. I know, because Chad told me.'

Neither of them brought up the possibility that either of the men might never return but would end up as a casualty of the war ... or worse. That was the stuff of nightmares, and neither of them wanted to think about those consequences.

Whilst the women were getting settled in, their men had moved out of the Southampton base. Brad and his men had joined up with the 82nd Airborne division and were to be dropped at Groesbeek, near Nijmegen. Neither man had jumped before, and so they had taken a crash course with some others. 'Remember to bend those knees as you land,' was the voice ringing in their ears as they climbed into the aircraft taking the troops to the drop zone.

'Give me a rodeo any time, even with a mad old steer!' Chad remarked as he lowered himself to the floor beside Brad.

'I've never ridden in a rodeo, but I've been to plenty, and to be honest, I'll take the jump!' was Brad's retort.

Operation Market Garden was under way. The objective was to take and hold three bridges. One at Eindhoven, one at Nijmegen and the other at Arnhem. British, American and Polish forces would all take part, hoping that with their might, and that of the allies already on the ground, their task would be completed.

The red light came on in the interior of the plane, and every man got to their feet and shuffled forward, clipped the line of their parachutes to the overhead apparatus – and waited. When the light changed to green, men tumbled out of the aircraft, one after another. Chad went just before Brad and he heard Chad let out a loud whoop.

'Crazy cowboy!' he muttered as his parachute opened and tugged at his shoulders.

As the troops landed and stowed their chutes, it appeared chaotic for a while until the men gathered and eventually found their companies with the road to Nijmegen stretched ahead of them. The plan was to scout out the town and reconnoitre the two bridges to be taken from the Germans and held. But the enemy was well established, and the troops were driven back time after time.

As the company took cover in any building they could find, the men took a break whilst the officers in charge talked with headquarters about their next move.

Chad pushed his helmet to the back of his head and lit a cigarette. He offered one to Brad, who took it gratefully. 'Thanks. Jeez, I'm glad that's over for a bit.'

Chad agreed. 'That was hairy, man! Any minute I expected a bullet to take me out.'

'I didn't have time to worry. We should have some extra might when the next drop arrives tomorrow and the gliders with the Poles come in. We need more firepower.'

'We need more everything!' Chad looked around. 'Did we lose many men?'

'A few, and if things don't improve, we'll lose a few more.'

'You're a bundle of laughs, Captain Jackson!'

'You have no idea the responsibility on my shoulders. I promised Jenny I'd bring you safely home.'

'You make damned sure you do, you hear? Oops, we're off again.' The men rose to their feet and gathered to make yet another attempt on the bridge.

'Come on, cowboy, you stick to me like glue.'

'I'm right behind you, Brad, so for Christ's sake keep your head down!'

The two women settled down at the house in Chilworth fairly quickly, neither encroaching on each other's privacy, yet coming together for meals and sharing the housework. Rusty knew nothing about gardening so was quickly shown the difference between a plant and a weed as she helped Jenny look after the outside.

As the days progressed, Jenny, now once more a resident at her old stomping ground, was surprised to find she was the centre of attention from several of the housewives in the area, who had learned about her friendship with the young GI. When they gathered together to plan a Winter Fête, with all the proceeds to go to the serving troops, this became very apparent.

After much discussion and planning, they broke for coffee, and two of the women wandered over to her.

'I suppose you're torn between the British and American troops when it comes to collecting funds and gifts for their well-being?'

Jenny frowned and looked puzzled. 'I beg your pardon?'

'Well, Jenny, we all know about you and the American horse whisperer.'

The second woman quickly interceded. 'Not that I blame you, darling, he's frightfully good-looking.'

The first woman was not so forgiving. 'I think it's disgusting! These Yanks come over here, they're overpaid and oversexed and women lose their heads – all for what?'

Jenny's hackles rose. 'You seem to be very well informed, Fiona – you tell me!'

The woman flushed. 'Very well, I will. Your husband is fighting for his country, and you are gallivanting around with another man – an American, at that. I think that's quite disgusting!'

'You can think what you like, Fiona, but frankly, what I do or don't do is none of your damned business, and I would appreciate you remembering that.'

'Well, I never did!'

'No, you probably never have, which is a great pity, it may have done you the world of good!' And she walked away, leaving the woman looking outraged.

Jenny stayed to the end of the meeting, as she had promised to help and felt duty bound to do so, but she was aware during the rest of the time there that several of the women were talking about her ... and now she knew why. Fiona Haskins, a leading light among the local women, had been made to look a fool and she didn't like it! She was now hell bent on revenge.

One of the women on the committee was Ethel Brown, the farmer's wife, a thoroughly down-to-earth woman. At the end of the meeting she walked over to Jenny, and taking her aside, she had a quiet word with her.

'Don't you take any notice of those busybodies with too much time on their hands! We all have but one life to live, and I know how things can happen to change it beyond all reasoning.' She then proceeded to tell her about her young friend Sarah and Gunter, the German prisoner of war.

Jenny listened with interest. She was used to hearing all kinds of stories at work from the women who would be sailing after the war to the States as GI brides, but this, with Gunter being German, had a different twist. 'How kind of you to take her in when she was pregnant,' Jenny said.

'What else could I do, Mrs Procter? He is a good man, and they're in love. That made the difference. He wants to marry her, it wasn't just a fling, but now I do have a problem.'

Seeing the worried expression on the woman's face, Jenny asked: 'What is it?'

'My son is coming home. He's been wounded, and now he hates the Germans, hasn't a good word to say about them, which is understandable. How do you think he'll feel about Sarah and her baby, fathered by a German? I don't know what to do.'

'Let's go and have a cup of tea somewhere and talk about this. Perhaps between us we can come up with an answer.'

A week later, Sarah and her baby moved into the house in Chilworth. When Sarah was made aware of Ethel Brown's predicament, she was only too pleased to fit in with any plans that would house her and the baby and give her a living.

Jenny had met Sarah at the farm soon after her chat with Ethel Brown and, liking the girl, had put a proposition to her: 'I need someone to keep the house clean. Rusty and I are out all day, so keeping the house and garden up to scratch takes up so much time – time that we really do not have. Everything is getting out of hand, and we'll never catch up. Are you interested in a live-in job for you and of course your baby?'

Sarah was delighted and had agreed immediately – and Rusty had insisted that as Jenny wouldn't let her pay any rent, she would pay half of Sarah's wage.

Once Sarah had settled in and worked out a routine, she wrote to Gunter explaining what had happened and telling him it was perfectly all right for him to write to her at this new address.

The baby in the house added a new dimension for Rusty and Jenny, and they both made a fuss of Hans when they were home, so Sarah had plenty of willing hands to help mother her child.

As Rusty said, 'I need to practice because Brad wants a family once we get married.'

They were all content in their way, which didn't sit well with Fiona Haskins. She had discovered Rusty's past and the fact that the young girl who was now living in and working for Jenny Procter had a child and was not yet married. The sanctimonious busybody began a campaign against them all.

Twenty-Two

It was Rusty who was the first to realize that something was going on. She was working on the haberdashery counter at Edwin Jones. It was a busy morning, but out of the corner of her eye, as she served several customers, she was aware that she seemed to be a subject of interest to two women. They were pretending to inspect the reels of cotton, but they seemed more interested in her. They watched her, then chatted to each other as they did so. It became somewhat unnerving, and eventually she walked over to them.

'Good morning, ladies, can I help you?'

Her direct approach threw them for a moment, and they scrambled to buy some elastic and cotton, following her to the counter with their goods. Whilst they waited for her to package their buys, one of them addressed her.

'Excuse me, miss, but aren't you staying with Mrs Procter?' one asked.

'Yes, I am.' Rusty looked somewhat puzzled.

The two women looked at each other with satisfied expressions. The taller of the two smirked and said, 'Chilworth is a bit out of your league, isn't it?'

Warning bells sounded loudly in Rusty's mind. She'd been around long enough to sense a predator, and this woman in particular was out to attack. 'I'm afraid I don't follow your line of questioning, madam.'

The woman glared at her. 'I would have thought Canal Walk would be more suitable for you!'

Rusty froze. Canal Walk was where she used to do her business when she was on the game. She stared straight at the woman and dearly longed to swipe the sly grin off her face. She wrapped the goods that had been bought, handed out the change, then she said very quietly, but with a note of steel in her voice, 'Here you are, madam, thank you very much. Carry them carefully, because I would be loath to have to shove the bag down your throat for casting aspersions on my character!'

The woman looked shocked. This certainly was not the reaction she had been expecting, and for a moment she was speechless.

'Thank you, good morning,' Rusty said and moved away to see to another customer. But behind her she could hear the two women's outrage as they eventually reacted to her remarks, although this time they kept their voices to a whisper as they walked away.

Rusty told Jenny all about this strange encounter as they drove home at the end of the day.

'What were they like?' Jenny asked. 'Describe them to me.' She listened and pursed her lips in anger. 'Did the taller one have a plummy accent?'

'Oh, yes,' agreed Rusty, 'and so condescending. She obviously forgets she has to go to the lavatory like we all do! I wanted to thump her, Jenny, honestly, I don't know how I kept my hands to myself.'

With a chuckle Jenny said, 'Oh Rusty, my dear, I've been wanting to do that for years. That obviously was Fiona Haskins. We have crossed swords many times, but we did so very recently. She dared to remark on my affair with Chad. She's a sanctimonious old bitch!'

'But a dangerous one, Jenny, make no mistake about that. She's out to make trouble. She's found out about my past somehow, and she knows about Chad. No doubt before long she'll learn that Sarah has a bastard child fathered by a German. The bloody woman will have a field day! Are there many occasions when the two of you have to be together?'

'We are on several committees. In fact she chairs two of them. Make no mistake, this woman has a great deal of sway in this community.'

Rusty sat and thought for a moment. 'What's the worst she could do to you?'

'Destroy my reputation, what's left of it. After I told Adam I wanted a divorce and why, I went about openly with Chad, but she could get me ostracized by the various committees, which would be a pity as I do feel I make a major contribution.'

'But that won't kill you, will it?'

'No, but I would be really annoyed if that was to happen, all because of a spiteful woman who thinks she's better than she is!'

Rusty began to smile. 'Listen, no one is guilt free. Everyone has a guilty pleasure – we just have to find out which one is hers!'

Jenny started giggling. 'Fiona Haskins with a guilty pleasure! Are you sure she'd even know what one was?'

'Trust me! In my business I've learned so much about people, and it's usually the last one you would suspect who is the worst. Fiona fits that bill to perfection. We just need to keep digging!'

The opportunity came sooner than either woman could have wished for. The following Sunday morning, Fiona Haskins was opening her house for a coffee morning, for charity. And when Rusty saw the advertisement in the local post-office window, she pointed it out to Jenny. 'Here we are. Old frosty face is having a do, and we need to attend.'

'Are you serious?' Jenny looked appalled.

'I'm deadly serious! We have to face the enemy and try and find out how well armed they are and search out their weak position. Oh my God! You can tell I've spent too long with the military can't you?' and she doubled up laughing.

'Are you prepared for whatever she throws at us? She won't be able to help herself, she'll *have* to have a dig at me. She wouldn't be able to resist the opportunity.'

Rusty stood tall and defiant. 'I can match her any time, and so can you. Come on, Jenny, let's strike a blow for freedom.'

'Yes, let's! The old trout *will* be surprised when we walk in.'

So it was on the following Sunday morning that Jenny and Rusty walked up the drive to Fiona Haskins' house and entered the open front door, following the arrows pointing to the room holding the coffee morning. It was very crowded.

'She's got a good turnout,' Rusty remarked.

'The Chilworth residents are very good when it comes to worthy causes,' Jenny told her, 'no matter who is holding the event.'

There was a table with two ladies serving coffee with boiling water from a large urn on a table at one end of the room; beside that, another table full of home-made cakes.

'Bloody hell!' Rusty exclaimed quietly. 'How did this lot happen with today's rationing?'

'I was wondering the same thing myself. It's really quite amazing.'

One or two of the local ladies started talking to Jenny, and Rusty slowly edged to the door. Once outside she found her way to the kitchen, just as someone emerged carrying yet another plate of cupcakes.

'I think I've died and gone to heaven!' Rusty

cried. 'I've never seen so many delicious cakes since war was declared.'

The woman beamed. 'I know, isn't it marvellous? We couldn't possibly do it without Fiona – she has ways and means of getting things done!' And she winked.

'I bet she has,' muttered Rusty, now alone in the kitchen. She opened the fridge and peered inside. There were several packets of butter beside a large slab of cheese, a dozen eggs and a leg of lamb. In the cupboard beside there was plenty of tea, American coffee ... and tinned fruit.

'Bloody hell! It looks as if she's raided a food warehouse.' Then she stood and smiled. 'Well, Fiona, this is your guilty pleasure! Gotcha!'

Rusty returned to the other room and sidled up to Jenny. 'I think it's time we tell our hostess just what a wonderful job she is doing, don't you? And don't forget to introduce me.' Seeing the look of concern Jenny gave her, she just grinned broadly. 'Trust me!'

They made their way carefully through the throng, clutching their coffee cups, until they found Fiona Haskins playing the lady bountiful in a loud voice.

'Fiona!' said Jenny, touching her arm.

The woman turned, and the smile froze on her lips.

'What a splendid turnout, you have done well. I believe you've already met my friend, Miss Dobbs?'

Rusty immediately spoke up. 'My goodness me, Mrs Haskins, I don't remember when I've seen such an array of cakes, and with rationing so very strict! All that butter and eggs needed for such a spread ... and you still have so much left! This coffee is delicious; I've not tasted as good except when an American gave me some from their stores.'

Fiona turned pale.

Rusty put a hand on her arm and leaned closer. 'But then I always say it's who you know rather than what you know, in such times as these.' And she tapped the side of her nose and winked at her before moving away, with Jenny quickly walking behind her.

'What the hell was all that about? I thought Fiona was about to pass out!'

'Well, my dear Jenny, our illustrious hostess is up to her neck in the black market. Oh my God!' Rusty stopped dead as a man emerged from one of the rooms.

'Jenny, my dear, how lovely to see you. How's it going in there?'

'Very well, James. Are you going to join them?'

'Not bloody likely! I'm off to my study.'

'This is my friend Rusty.' But Rusty had walked away and was already halfway down the drive.

James Haskins followed her gaze and saw the redhead in the distance. 'Never mind, I'll meet her another time. Good to see you. Have you heard from Adam?'

'Not lately, but you know how difficult it is for mail to get through, then several letters arrive at the same time.'

'Well, take care, Jenny. Good to see you.'

She ran down the path to catch up with her friend. 'Why did you take off like that?'

'That man used to be one of my clients. What was he doing there?'

Jenny tried not to smile. 'How absolutely priceless! That is James, Fiona's husband!'

'No!'

'Yes, I'm afraid he is.'

'Oh, don't be afraid, Jenny, he was one of my favourites, a great lover. With him it was my pleasure, believe me!'

They both walked down the drive, their laughter echoing.

At the study window, James Haskins watched them and smiled softly to himself as he remembered.

His reverie was interrupted by his wife, who swept into the room in high dudgeon. She stormed around the room, complaining loudly about having her privacy invaded. Then, eventually, she sat down.

When James inquired as to the cause of her fury, she told him about Rusty's remarks.

Her husband chuckled. 'I did warn you about dealing in the black market, and you dismissed me, if I recall.'

'And that Jenny Procter has a cheek to show up here when we all know about her and that American GI!'

James looked intrigued. 'Are you implying that's she's having an affair?'

'I'm not implying anything, it's a well-known fact!'

'Then good for her! I could never understand what she was doing with that pompous oaf Procter; she deserves much better.'

215

'James! What a terrible thing to say.'

'Not at all, my dear, and my advice to you is people in glass houses shouldn't throw stones. Just hope that Jenny's friend, that glamorous redhead, doesn't tell the authorities about you!' And he walked out of the room.

Twenty-Three

The men of the 82nd Airborne division were weary. Despite the fact that eighty per cent of their supplies had been recovered from several drops, the weather had deteriorated, stopping vital troops from gliding in. The company still had been unable to capture the bridge at Nijmegen and were now fighting to take control of the landing zone.

That evening, as Brad and Chad sat eating their K rations, they both admitted how tired they were.

'I'm beat,' said Chad as he lit a cigarette. 'God, I thought I was a really fit man, but I've never ever been so damned tired.'

Brad pushed his helmet to the back of his head and rubbed his eyes. 'Me too, buddy. What I wouldn't give for a hot bath and a comfortable bed. I'd sell my soul to the devil for it, given the opportunity!'

'No, you wouldn't, you're one of the good guys!'

Brad started laughing. 'Whatever gave you that idea?'

'I've gotten to know you pretty well since we came to Britain, but don't let it go to your head!'

Brad looked across at his friend. He had been made up to sergeant now and was very popular with the men. His way of handling them was different. He didn't yell or shout at them, there were no snide remarks about their inabilities as soldiers – he just showed them respect and understanding. No doubt helped by his experiences with horses, he understood the men's psyches. Nevertheless, when it was necessary, Chad could yell as well as the next sergeant.

The two men had been firm friends before they were sent to the war zone, but in battle real friendships are forged which last a lifetime, and these two men looked out for each other through friendship and mutual admiration.

They spent the rest of the evening talking about their plans for the future.

'When eventually I get my ranch up and running,' Chad said, 'you and Rusty ought to come out and stay for a vacation. After all, you're not that far away. The girls would love to spend some time together there.'

'That'd be great,' agreed Brad. 'Like you, I'll have to take time to set up my practice again.'

'But what about the patients that you had before. Won't they come back?'

'I doubt it! You forget how long it's been. They will, by now, feel comfortable with their new practitioner. The doctor-patient relationship is very personal, and that's important both for the doctor and the patient.'

'There you go,' Chad remarked with a grin.

'You're a people whisperer!'

Shaking his head, Brad smiled. 'How that lovely woman puts up with you, I'll never know!'

'To be honest, Brad, neither do I, but thank God she does. I feel the luckiest guy on the planet. Right, I'm off to get some sleep, see you in the morning. Let's hope it's an easier day than today.' And he made his way to his bed.

Back at home, Jenny and Rusty got on with their lives, watching the post every morning in the hopes of hearing from their men. When a letter did arrive, the recipient would go off in a quiet corner to read the contents before sharing whatever news with the other. Like their two men, they'd become firm friends and cheered each other when one felt low.

This particular evening, they were in the sitting room exchanging gossip when the telephone rang. 'Who on earth can that be?' Jenny said as she went to answer it. 'Yes, this is Jenny Procter. Yes, my husband is Captain Adam Procter.'

Rusty looked up and saw the shocked expression on Jenny's face.

'Where did you say he was?' Jenny listened for a moment and then asked: 'Can I go and see him?' After taking down some details, she replaced the receiver.

'Jenny! Whatever is the matter? You look terrible.'

She sank into the chair beside the phone. 'It's Adam! He's been injured and is in hospital.'

'Oh my God! Is he badly hurt?'

'They wouldn't say, just asked if I would go and see him and talk to his doctor.'

'Where is he?'

'In a military hospital in Basingstoke. I must find out the train times. I'll go up in the morning.'

'I'm coming with you!' said Rusty.

'But your job?'

'I'll ring in the morning. You can't go alone. Who knows what's happened!' She walked over to Jenny and put a comforting arm around her. 'Maybe it won't be too bad.'

Neither of the women slept well that night, wondering what they would face the following day. They left Southampton in the morning and eventually arrived at the hospital.

Jenny went up to the reception desk and spoke to the nurse on duty. 'I'm Mrs Jenny Procter. I received a call last night to say that my husband, Captain Adam Procter, had been brought here. I would like to see him, please.'

'One moment, Mrs Procter,' said the nurse and looked through several notes on her desk. She frowned and said, 'Yes, that's right, just one moment please.' She made a call to tell someone of Jenny's arrival, then asked her to take a seat for a moment.

As they sat waiting, Rusty took hold of Jenny's hand and squeezed it, but neither said a word.

Before very long they heard the sound of footsteps and saw a man wearing a white coat approaching. 'Which of you is Mrs Procter?' he asked.

Jenny stood up. 'I am.'

'Would you like to come with me, please?'

'I'd like my friend to come too. Is that all right?'

'Yes, of course,' he said quietly, 'just follow me.'

Jenny could feel her heart racing as she followed the man. He showed her into what appeared to be his consulting room and indicated that they should take a seat.

'I am Dr Braxton and have been attending to your husband.'

'Is he badly injured?' asked Jenny fearfully.

'I'm afraid so. He was injured by an explosion. He has mainly superficial injuries caused by shrapnel, but I'm so sorry to have to tell you that, due to the blast, he is blind.'

Jenny let out a cry of anguish and covered her mouth with her hand.

'Oh my God!' exclaimed Rusty.

'Is this a permanent thing?' asked Jenny. 'Is there any hope that he may regain his sight?'

'I'm afraid not. The optic nerves have been too badly damaged.'

Jenny sat, stunned by the news, unable to fully grasp the situation.

'What happens to Captain Procter now?' asked Rusty.

'He'll remain a patient here for a while until we can get him well. As you can imagine, he's been through a series of operations where we tried to save his sight and he's a sick man at the moment. When he's well enough, we'll send him to St Dunstan's, where they will train him to cope without his sight and teach him Braille – then he'll come home.'

'What sort of a life will he have then? He'll not be able to work, he'll have a terrible time. He'll hate every moment! You don't know my husband, Dr Braxton.' Jenny was beside herself with worry.

'He'll need a great deal of help, Mrs Procter, to get used to being blind. But you know it is possible to lead a good life if you are mentally strong. But I won't lie to you, it isn't going to be easy.'

'Can I see him?' asked Jenny.

'Yes, of course, but I would ask you not to stay too long, not this time. I'm sure it will cheer the captain to hear your voice, but I don't want him tired. I'm sure you understand.'

'Of course.'

'I'll show you to his room. He's in a side ward where he can be quiet. Your friend can sit in the waiting room.'

Jenny tried to fight off the trepidation she felt as she was taken to see Adam. She had no idea what she was about to face.

At the door, the doctor left her. 'Half an hour at the longest,' he told her.

Jenny opened the door. The smell of ether and disinfectant seemed to invade her nostrils, making her feel nauseous. She stepped inside the room.

Adam was lying in bed, his eyes covered with bandages. He looked frail and thin. She walked over to the bed and gently took his hand. 'Adam, it's Jenny.'

He stirred just a little and moved his head straining to listen. 'Jenny, is that really you?'

'Yes, Adam, I'm so sorry to see you like this.'

'I wondered if you would come,' he said weakly. 'Thank you, it means so much to me.'

She could tell that talking was wearying him.

221

'Don't talk,' she said. 'They will only let me stay for a while.'

He squeezed her hand. 'Next time you can perhaps stay a little longer.' His voice faded, and he fell asleep.

She sat studying her husband. This was so unlike the man she knew. Adam had been a *tour de force;* now he looked weak and frail. How on earth would he be able to cope in the future? Thirty minutes later, she gently removed her hand from his and crept out of the room.

Rusty was walking up and down the waiting room, worried for her friend, wondering what was going to happen next. She stopped as Jenny walked in and held her friend as she dissolved into tears.

When Jenny had recovered, she told her friend about Adam. 'He looked so ill, it was all he could do to say a few words. Oh Rusty, what a terrible thing to happen to him. His life is in ruins!'

Although Rusty felt sympathy for the man lying in the hospital bed, she was more concerned about Jenny. *And your life is also in ruins,* she thought to herself.

The train journey home was taken in almost complete silence, both women sat lost in their own thoughts. Rusty anxiously watched her friend, whose shoulders were slumped and her face pale.

Jenny was trying to face the facts that had just been put before her, seeing her future happiness slowly and painfully fading away. 'I can't possibly leave him now!' she suddenly exclaimed and then burst into tears.

Rusty put an arm round Jenny, but couldn't find the words to comfort her. What could she say? What would she do if she was in that position? She honestly didn't know. If only Brad was here! With his medical background he would be able to assess the situation rationally. She felt completely hopeless and helpless.

Once they arrived at Southampton, they took a taxi home. Rusty put the kettle on and then poured Jenny a stiff brandy. 'Here, drink this, it's good for shock.' She poured herself one too, then made a pot of tea.

'There's no sense in making any decision until you know more about Adam's situation,' she said as she poured the steaming liquid into a cup.

'What more is there to know?' said Jenny. 'Adam is blind. He couldn't possibly manage without help for the rest of his life. How can I walk away from him, knowing that?'

'What about Chad, your plans for the future? Are you going to throw that all away?'

'What choice do I have? I *have* no choice!' she cried.

'Stop that!' Rusty shook Jenny by the shoulders. 'All your married life, Adam has made decisions for you. Now, you have to fight for what you want.' She stood up and stalked around the kitchen angrily. 'For Christ's sake, Jenny, for the first time in your life, stand up for yourself! Don't throw in the towel so easily!'

'You didn't see Adam or you wouldn't be so heartless!'

Rusty drew up a chair beside her. 'Look at me!' she demanded.

Somewhat startled by the ferocious tone of her voice, Jenny did as she was told.

'Don't think for one minute I'm not deeply sorry for Adam, because I am. My heart goes out to him, but I am more concerned about you at this moment. Adam will get the best medical treatment going, and though this may sound hard, he's not the first man to lose his sight. He'll be trained to cope, as have many others, and in time he will have a quality to his life – not the one he had hoped for, but a life that can be lived. But you ... *you* will be destroyed! Now, that's not right in any man's language.'

'I know what you say is true, but I don't know if I'll be strong enough to walk away when the time comes.'

'At least give some consideration to the man who adores you!' Rusty let out a sigh of frustration. 'Chad will be devastated if you let him down. How can you live with that?'

'I'm not at all sure that I can. Oh Rusty – what a mess!'

'You listen to me. You'll have to see Adam, of course you will. He needs you now, and because of the years you've been together, you have to help him at this time.' She caught hold of Jenny's hand and gripped it tightly. 'But never *ever* let him think this is a permanent situation! If at any time he talks as if he thinks it is, you must gently remind him of your plans. Don't give him any false hopes. That way you'll be able to cope and he will be prepared for it.'

'You should be a psychologist! Where did you learn all this?'

Rusty chuckled. 'Mostly on my back, darling!'

Despite everything, Jenny had to laugh. 'Do you think I should write to Chad and explain the situation?'

Rusty looked appalled. 'What, and worry him to death? What would be the point? Goodness knows *when* the men will be home. Until that time you can do your duty by Adam, help get him on his feet, and then later, when this bloody war is over, we can all get on with our lives.'

'Thank goodness we met and became friends, Rusty, I'd be lost without you.'

'And where would I be at this moment if we'd not met? It was fate that brought us all together, and together we'll stay!'

'You are an extraordinary woman!'

Rusty just raised her eyebrows and smiled. 'So I've been told in the past!'

'And naughty!'

'That too! But I'm a survivor, I've had to be, but I've learned to fight for what I believe is right, and you must do the same. Do you think that Adam would want you to stay with him out of pity?'

'In the beginning I don't think he'd care as long as I was there, but later, no, he'd hate it ... and what's more he'd let me know it.'

'And then you will have given up everything for nothing!'

'I'll just have to take it one step at a time, that's all.'

'Then we'll take those steps together, Jenny, because I'm not sure I trust you to be strong!'

Jenny Procter didn't answer, but she knew that

Rusty spoke the truth. She would feel it was her sense of duty to stay with Adam, and she needed someone to push her when the time came. How lucky she was, she thought, to have found such a friend.

Twenty-Four

The next two months were difficult for everybody. Adam battled with his health; Jenny tried to help by visiting twice a week, and more if she could get away from her job with the forces. When she tried to explain to her husband that she was working, sorting out the papers and details of the GI brides, he was scathing.

'That is more important than coming here to see me?'

'I have to make a living, and I'm paid to do this job ... and I feel it's worthwhile.'

'You don't have to work! How many times must I tell you this? I will provide financially for you!'

Jenny breathed deeply to try and remain calm. 'Adam, there is no need to do so, especially under the circumstances.'

He put his hand up to the bandages covering his eyes in frustration. 'If only I could bloody well see, then we could talk sensibly!'

Thinking of Rusty and her advice, Jenny tried to be firm. 'Adam, not being able to see me makes no difference. You know what I mean, and nothing has changed.'

He cursed loudly. 'For me, *everything* has changed. For Christ's sake, woman, how can you sit there and say that?'

'That's not what I mean, and you know it.' She got up and walked to the window. She knew that it was never going to be easy, but why did it have to be *so* difficult? Then she chided herself for being so selfish; after all, she wasn't the one in the hospital bed. But how to handle Adam and at the same time be of help was beyond her. She decided to have a word with the doctor before she left and see what he had to say.

Dr Braxton tried to reassure Jenny. 'The first few months are the worst. I promise it will get better in time, but, to begin with, the realization that you will never be able to see again is a terrible thing. There is desolation, anger, frustration ... and, eventually, acceptance. That's when we can really get to work and start rehabilitation. St Dunstan's comes in to its own then. In time the patient realizes that there is a sort of light at the end of the tunnel, even if they can't see one, and that all is not lost – then it's up to the individual.'

'How do you think my husband will cope, Doctor?'

The man shook his head. 'It's very difficult to say, Mrs Procter. If your marriage is a strong one, that'll help.'

Jenny's heart sank. 'I feel you should know all the facts, Doctor Braxton, as it might help in my husband's treatment. We are separated. I plan to get a divorce and move to the States when the war finally ends.'

'Ah.' The doctor smiled softly. 'That would

explain his extreme anger. He's not only lost his sight, but you also.'

'I know, and don't think I don't feel guilty about this, because I do. We were married for a long time.'

'Forgive me, but I have to know – is there any chance that you might change your mind and stay with the captain?'

Shaking her head, Jenny said, 'No. At first I felt it was my duty to do so, but it just won't work. The war changes us all, and I'm afraid although I have a deep affection for him, I no longer love my husband. I know that once we were home together, then the rot would set in, and that wouldn't be good for Adam.'

'Then I suggest, Mrs Procter, that you don't visit the captain so often. The sooner he gets used to the idea that you won't be around, the sooner we can rehabilitate him. Now he's just confused and no doubt thinks that you will eventually stand by him, which will only make it harder for him when you leave for good.'

Jenny felt like a traitor. To walk away from Adam at such a time seemed cruel in the extreme. She looked at the man sitting opposite and met his gaze. 'Are you sure this is the way to go?'

'Absolutely positive. Forgive me for being blunt, but if you are leaving your husband for another man, the sooner you go the better for him.'

'You make it sound so callous! I was married to Adam for nineteen years, but I fell in love with an American. It wasn't planned, it just happened.

228

Then this! Believe me, Doctor Braxton, I have been torn between the devil and the deep, but I know getting on with my life will ultimately be the right thing for both of us.'

'I'm not here to judge you, Mrs Procter; I'm just interested in what's best for my patient. Captain Procter will soon be moved to St Dunstan's, and I suggest you give him a month before you visit, which doesn't mean you can't write – a nurse will read out your letters to him – but please don't give him any false hopes about the future.'

Jenny rose from her seat and shook the doctor's hand. 'Thank you, you have been very helpful.'

The next three months flew by, and December was soon upon them. Adam was now at St Dunstan's and seemed at last to be settling down to a new regime. He was becoming more adept at walking around unaided once he knew the layout of his surroundings, which gave him a feeling of independence, and whenever Jenny did visit him he seemed more cheerful. But each time she saw him he told her he couldn't wait to come home, which filled her with a certain amount of trepidation as to how he would manage. Once again, Adam would have to hire staff to take care of him. In her heart, Jenny knew that Adam was hoping she would step into the breach, that her feeling of duty would overcome everything else.

Brad and Chad were still in Holland but no longer near Arnhem. It had been a bridge too far, and the American troops had had to retreat, eventually. The company had tried to cross the

229

river to get to the bridge, but they'd had to use British boats, with which they were unfamiliar; there was also a shortage of paddles, which didn't help their cause. The men were using rifle butts in some cases, but the covering fire was heavy and the men had to fall back. As they did so, they were trapped in a pocket of land, with no possibility of escaping. They dug themselves in as quickly as possible.

Brad called for the radio operator and reported his position, hoping for covering gunfire; they were not in any position to help, but he was told that more troops would be sent to aid them.

Brad could hear Chad giving orders to his men as they returned fire, keeping their heads down as the bullets whizzed past them. They continued to hold their position until eventually more troops arrived with their added firepower. It was a great relief, and they were able to fall back to safety.

The two men had survived, and they wrote to the women they loved when they were able – never telling them of their narrow escape, of course, but about their hopes for the future, and about how the war could not possibly last for much longer.

Rusty liked to curl up in a chair and try to visualize her future. She had nothing to leave behind that meant anything at all to her, except perhaps for the friendship of Jenny Procter, but they would be in the same country and nearby states. They had vowed to keep in touch with each other once they were in America. It was a kind of safety line which they both would protect and treasure.

The girls had spoken about finding another flat to share now that Adam was back in England, but he wouldn't hear of it.

'How ridiculous! I've no idea how long I'll be at St Dunstan's, and in any case, the house is enormous, there's certainly room for us all. Besides, I'm not sure how long it'll be before I'm allowed home for good, so the house must be occupied when I'm not there.'

Jenny had finally agreed, with the understanding that once Adam was back home permanently, they would move out.

Christmas came at last. Jenny and Rusty spent the holiday at Beth's, helping with the horses and enjoying a family Christmas after all. On Boxing Day they all went out for a ride early in the morning through the woods, which looked like a fairyland with the hoar frost making the ferns look magical.

Jenny looked across at Rusty, sitting on her mount with confidence, and grinned at her friend. 'If Brad could see you now, he would be surprised. You sit there as if you know what you're doing!'

'I need to practice for when we are back at his place! You know how he loves to ride.'

'You'll be joining the hunt before you know it!' Jenny teased.

'Not bloody likely! I've watched the hunt in action; when a fox has been sighted, it's crazy. Everyone is off like a shot, jumping anything that gets in the way. That's too bloody dangerous for me, thank you!'

During the first week of January, Adam came home for a week to see how he would be able to cope. He had a male nurse in attendance who walked him round every room to familiarize him once again with the contents of his home.

During this time, Sarah took Hans to stay at Beth's. It was deemed too complicated to have Sarah stay, with little Hans running around and perhaps tripping Adam up, and Jenny wasn't sure how Adam would feel about having them living there, anyway.

Once he was settled in, on the day of his arrival, the nurse had a word with Jenny. 'Whatever you do, Mrs Procter, don't move any furniture or your husband could trip over it and hurt himself,' he told Jenny. 'He will have memorized everything in its place, and there it must stay.'

'I understand,' she told him.

It was an uncomfortable time for them all. Rusty felt she was intruding, Jenny felt even guiltier about leaving Adam, and Adam became more and more demanding as each day passed.

'I don't know where you get your patience from,' Jenny said to Jack the male nurse after Adam had been particularly unpleasant one morning.

'Ah well, Mrs Procter, I know my patient. He's proud, and now he feels less of a man because he's unable to see and so is not in control. And he's angry – even more so because of the state of his marriage, if you forgive me for saying so.'

'He's told you about us?' Jenny asked with surprise.

'Oh yes. In the beginning when the captain was

232

first injured, he talked to me a lot. I think it was the only way he could cope. After all, he can't see me; that makes it so much easier to open up. If he was sighted, he would never have done so.'

'Yes, I understand.'

'What perhaps you don't understand, Mrs Procter, is that your husband honestly believes that when push comes to shove you'll stay with him. But that's not how you see it, is it?'

Jenny was horrified. 'I thought I made it very clear to Adam that my plans hadn't changed.'

'Oh, you did that, but you see that's not what he wants to hear, so he refuses to accept the fact. I have tried to make him see he's barking up the wrong tree, but he doesn't want to know.'

'What can I do about it?'

'Move out of the house. As long as you are installed here, the captain thinks you'll stay for good.'

'Thank you, Jack. When Adam returns to St Dunstan's, I'll find a flat.'

'It'll be for the best, Mrs Procter, in the long run.'

The following morning, Adam had just finished his breakfast when he heard the front doorbell ring. 'I'll go, Jack,' he said, pushing his chair back and reaching for his white stick. He liked to greet the postman these days and open the front door to those who called. He was feeling more confident in his own surroundings and wanted to show those who knew him that he could manage perfectly well, thank you!

'That you, postman?' he asked as he opened the

door. 'Got anything interesting for me today?'

'Good morning, Captain Procter. I'm afraid I'm not the postman.'

Adam froze for a moment as he heard the American accent.

'It's Chad Maxwell; we met once before at the stables.'

'You're that bloody cowboy!'

There was a note of amusement in the American's voice when he answered. 'Well, sir, I guess you could put it like that.'

'What do you want?' Adam was brusque.

'I've called to see Jenny. I flew in from France a couple of hours ago and have to fly out again tonight.'

'There's no point in you seeing her, my man. As you can see I'm home now, and Jenny is taking care of me. She has decided that she needs to be with me, so any thoughts you might have of a future together with my wife, I'm afraid, are out of the question. She's decided her place is here with me.'

Chad was stunned. He had been taken by surprise when the door was opened by Adam; then to see that he was blind, and now to be told that Jenny had decided to stay with her husband! She'd not written about Adam in her letters. Those had been full of love and affection, talking about their future together. What on earth was going on? 'Where is Jenny now?' Chad demanded.

'I have no idea,' Adam lied. 'She's away for the day and won't be back until this evening.'

'Leaving you alone?' he asked suspiciously.

'No, I have a male nurse in attendance to give

Jenny a hand. As you can imagine, this takes some getting used to, and it would be too much to expect her to take me on by herself.'

'And where is Rusty? She and Jenny were staying here together; at least, that was what I was told in her letters.'

'Yes, that's right. Until I came home, of course, then she moved out to a flat.'

'Do you have her address?'

'What on earth would I want that for? Now, if you'll excuse me, I've to take some medication. I'm sorry things didn't work out for you, but frankly, I think it was only a temporary aberration on my wife's part. It was never going to last – you know how it is in wartime.' Adam turned away and closed the door.

Twenty-Five

Chad stood looking at the closed door, his mind in a whirl. He had been taken completely by surprise to see Adam and was shocked when he realized the poor guy was blind! How dreadful for him – and for Jenny. He'd been moving around France these past few weeks and hadn't received any mail from her, no doubt telling him about Adam's condition. But had she really thrown away a future with him to look after her husband, after everything they'd been to each other? As he walked to the jeep he told the driver to take him to the stables and gave him directions. Beth would know what was going on.

But when he arrived, it was to discover that Beth was away and wouldn't be back until that evening. There was no one there that he knew and could ask about Jenny. Unfortunately, Brad had been seconded to another company several weeks ago, so his other means of communication were closed. Rusty would have told Brad of any change in Jenny's plans.

On the way back to the camp, he got the driver to stop at a florist's, where he ordered flowers for Jenny. On the card he wrote: *Sorry I missed you today, darling. Will be in touch. Love you like crazy. Chad xx*

He had to let her know that, for him, nothing had changed.

When the flowers were delivered, Jack took them to Adam. 'These flowers have just arrived for Mrs Procter. What shall I do with them?'

'Is there a card with them?'

'Yes, sir.'

'Open it and read it to me.'

Jack did so, and when he'd finished, Adam calmly said, 'Take them outside and put them in the dustbin! They never arrived, you understand?'

'Yes, sir.'

It was in Jenny's best interests, Adam told himself. Her obsession with this young man would pass; it was a wartime madness. She belonged with him in this house, and he'd be damned if he would let her waste her life with a bloody cowboy! But beneath his veneer, Adam was scared.

Without Jenny, he didn't think he could cope. He realized, too, that his behaviour had been unreasonable during some of his stay, which was not the way to win her over.

Jenny, unaware of all the drama at Chilworth, was visiting a letting agency during her lunch hour. She'd told Rusty what Jack, the male nurse had advised, and her friend was only too pleased to move.

'To be honest, Jenny,' Rusty had said, 'I've felt very uncomfortable being in the house with Adam. I really felt I was intruding. But if he's still determined to keep you by his side, then Jack is right to suggest you move out.'

Jenny looked at a few flats and told the agent she'd bring her friend to look them over before deciding. One or two of them were perfectly adequate, as far as she was concerned, but Rusty would have to agree, it was only fair.

Knowing that Rusty had plans to visit friends that evening, Adam had Jack order dinner from a restaurant, delivered to the door. Jack laid the table and found two candlesticks and candles and set it out in readiness. When Jenny walked through the front door, the nurse informed her that dinner would be served in half an hour.

Taken somewhat by surprise, and feeling decidedly weary, she just smiled and said, 'How nice, I'll go and freshen up.'

When she eventually sat at the dining room table with Adam, she had to admit he handled eating his food very well. Jack told him where everything was on his plate, as if the plate was a clock face. His meat at eight o'clock, his potatoes at four, etc. Then he left them alone.

Jenny had forgotten how charming Adam could be. She enjoyed the chicken and the dessert and found herself relaxing in the familiarity that the years spent together had fostered. Adam was recounting old scenarios that had caused them both such hilarity in times gone by.

He turned his head in her direction. 'It wasn't all bad, Jenny, was it?'

'No, of course not.' She gazed at her husband. He was still handsome; his hair greying at the temples made him look distinguished, and when he smiled she remembered the young man she'd fallen in love with so long ago. It broke her heart to see him now, dependent on others most of the time. She did realize that, as each week passed, Adam was becoming more confident and able to do more for himself, but he was a selfish man and she knew that, without a doubt, whoever was with him would be at his beck and call continuously – but it had been fun to reminisce.

Adam leaned forward towards her. 'Jenny, darling, don't throw what we had away. We can still have a good life together.'

The atmosphere of the evening changed in seconds. What had been fun and easy now became tense and edgy.

'Please, Adam, let's not go there. If this was your plan – to soften me up with dinner, candlelight and reminiscences about old times to get me to stay with you – then sadly it was all for nothing. It's a pity because, until now, I was enjoying it all.'

She rose from the table. 'I'm off to bed. Thank you for the meal.'

Adam listened to her retreating footsteps and cursed to himself. He couldn't let her go without a fight. She was his wife, and they had spent too many years together to have some young Yank come along and ruin everything! He lit a cigarette. Was it about sex – was that what made the whole thing so exciting? But they had had a good sex life he had always thought.

But when he stopped to really think about it, it hadn't been special. Whenever he felt like it, he would reach for Jenny in bed. She rarely refused, and he was always satisfied, job done!

He stubbed his cigarette out angrily. Women! No man could ever understand them.

Upstairs in her bedroom, Jenny undressed and thought about the previous few hours. What a shame the whole dinner had been part of a plan, instead of just two people enjoying a meal and good conversation. But that was typical of Adam. He was always insistent on getting his own way; it was the manner of the man. As long as he was satisfied, that was what counted. It was the same in bed. Once Adam had reached his climax, nothing else mattered, he would turn over and sleep, whereas Chad was so thoughtful as a lover, making sure that she too was satisfied. How she longed for him at this moment.

It wasn't until the following morning that Beth was told about the American GI who had been asking for her. When Beth asked for a description of the soldier, she realized that it had to be Chad.

She immediately rang Jenny at her office. 'So did you see Chad yesterday?' Beth asked as soon as Jenny answered the phone.

'What are you talking about?'

'A GI came looking for me yesterday, but I was out. His description fitted Chad so I was sure you had seen him.'

'No, I left the house early in the morning and didn't get back until late.' She hesitated, then swore softly.

'What is it?' asked Beth.

'Last night Adam arranged a candlelight dinner as a surprise to tempt me back, and now I know why. Chad must have gone to the house. Oh my God! What must he have thought to see Adam there?'

'That all depends if he saw Adam and if they spoke, I suppose.'

'If they did, I can imagine what was said. Adam is such a devious sod! He'd do anything to keep me here.'

'If that was the case, Chad would wait until he saw you, I'm sure, before believing any story. You just have to wait until you hear from him.'

'I can't do anything else, but I shall certainly have a word with Adam when I go home tonight. He can't run my life for me, and it's time to remind him of that!'

Adam was sitting by the fire in the living room, sipping a glass of brandy, when Jenny swept into the room that evening, bristling with indignation. 'So what lies did you tell Chad when he called?' she demanded.

At first he was startled, but then he just smiled. 'How did you find out he'd called?'

'He went looking for Beth. What did you say to him, Adam?'

'I told him you had decided to stay with me.'

'You what? How dare you! You had no right to do such a thing, and it was a lie.'

'At the moment it is, but I know you'll soon come to your senses. Then it'll be the truth.'

She couldn't believe what she was hearing. 'When will you accept that our marriage is over? Even if I never heard from Chad again, I wouldn't come back to you, Adam. You are a selfish, self-centred, controlling man who has never learned about humility, even now. I'm moving the rest of my stuff out tomorrow. You will need to arrange for someone else to care for the house. I no longer want anything to do with it – or you!'

The following day, Jenny and Rusty moved into a flat in Hill Lane. She went to the Post Office to fill in a form for change of address, as she didn't want any of her mail to go to the house. Adam was not to be trusted with any letters that might come from Chad, and now more than ever she needed to hear from her lover to find out if he believed Adam's lies.

She sat down before she went to bed and wrote a long letter to Chad, assuring him that she still loved him.

Nothing will come between us, my darling, she wrote. *At one time, I confess, I thought it was my duty to stay with Adam, but it wouldn't work, and I would wilt away to nothing without you beside me. I can't wait for this terrible war to be over so we can start our life together. Yours always, Jenny xxx*

She prayed that Chad would receive the letter in the near future.

But Chad Maxwell was on an aircraft, flying to France once again. He had delivered his papers into the right hands and now was returning to his company. Surely this damned war had to be over soon? He couldn't wait to get out of uniform, back on a horse and the open country side without the sound of gunfire ... with the woman he loved.

He wondered just where Brad was at this time. He really missed his company. He put his head back, closed his eyes and slept.

But at the stables, no one was asleep. Little Hans had become very poorly in the early evening, and his condition had worsened. Here, everyone was awake ... and worried.

Twenty-Six

Captain Brad Jackson was war weary, as was every man in his company. They all wanted to pack up and go home to their families and a normal life. But, for many, normality would never be the case. So many servicemen would have their lives altered for ever, due to the injuries they received during the fighting. And, for some of them, death would have been kinder. Brad had to deal with these men and try and get them up and give them some kind of hope before he shipped them home.

As a doctor, he knew that it wasn't only his injured men who were the ones to suffer. Depending on the extent of the injuries, some of the soldiers' family members couldn't cope with sons or husbands who would return as different people, not the fit and healthy men they once knew.

Some of the men were courageous and mentally strong, accepting that things would never be the same, but determined to make the most of the help that was offered by the service hospitals, but others were unable to see a future and felt they had lost their livelihood and, consequently, their manhood.

In Southampton, Jenny was doing a similar job but with less brutal injuries. Some of the women who came into her office were in dire straits. Not all the women had been married to their GIs before they were sent to the battlefields, and many of them had illegitimate children to show for their liaisons with the men. Those who suffered most were the women with Negro babies. In many southern states of America it was illegal for a Negro to mix with a white woman, and to give her a child was a lynching offence.

In their own hometown, the women were looked down upon, and now they had no financial support from the father. This was the hardest part of Jenny's job, but she did what she could for the women, using the WVS to help with clothing for the babies, and begging, borrowing or stealing anything else she could from any organization that she thought could help.

Three weeks had passed since Chad had called, but Jenny had not heard from him. She couldn't imagine what was in his mind after calling at the house and seeing Adam there. Would he really have believed that she was back with her husband?

Rusty hadn't had a letter from Brad either, but it wasn't surprising – the war in Europe was still raging, but slowly the Germans were being beaten, and the bombing of Dresden had put fear into the hearts of the German people.

Eventually, in March, the US Army crossed the Rhine at Remagen. Brad was with the army as it finally drove over the bridge, which had been detonated by the Germans but had failed to explode. When General Bradley realized the fact, he sent everything he could across it.

A letter from Rusty had eventually caught up with Brad, but it had been written some time before, so he was unaware of Adam's status and the brief visitation of his buddy. But now the allies were across the Rhine and the Russians rapidly approaching Berlin, the general consensus of opinion was that the end was nigh, and Brad was content to wait to catch up with the woman he loved.

In the prisoner of war camp, Gunter listened to the news every night, praying for the end of the fighting so he could be repatriated and prepare a

244

home for his family. He had written to his parents, but had not received a reply. They could be with his sister – or worse, beneath a pile of rubble. He had no way of knowing until he was able to return to Germany and see for himself.

In the camp, most of the prisoners realized that Germany was losing the war. Most by now just wanted it to end so they could be free, but the few dyed-in-the-wool Nazis were very bitter, and when, in April, Hitler committed suicide in a bunker in Berlin, they felt cheated and betrayed ... but Gunter was filled with hope.

Chad was in Prague with the US Third Army when it took the city, but they were ordered to stay there to allow the Russians to take the rest of the country. None of the servicemen cared. They were happy to settle in for the time being, away from the fighting.

Chad sat quietly in a corner of a small cafe he had found, with a small glass of brandy which the owner had proudly produced as Chad sat at the table.

'God Bless America!' the man cried and grinning all over his face disappeared into the back.

Chad chuckled to himself and started a letter to Jenny.

Hello, darling. We are in Prague, and the fighting is over for a time and hopefully for good before too long. I've been moving around so have received no mail at all. I was in the UK briefly a few months ago and called at your house. I saw Adam. Poor guy, what a rotten shame. He told me that you were staying with

245

him. I can understand that you think you have a duty to this man who you were married to for so long, but I am praying that you still want to be with me and come and live in Wyoming.

This makes me sound like a heel, with Adam being blind and all, but Jenny honey, I love you so much, and I can't bear to think of you dying inside as you surely would if you stayed in Chilworth with him.

I may not make it back to see you if an armistice is declared in the near future. I may be shipped home first to be discharged, but I want you to know, I'm coming back for you, darling, however long it takes.

Yours always and forever,
Chad.

At last the war was over. There was dancing in the streets, street parties, the pubs were bursting at the seams with people celebrating VE day. But there were many who celebrated with heavy hearts. Pleased that the fighting was over, but knowing that their lives would never be the same again.

Rusty, Jenny and Sarah all celebrated at the stables with Beth. Sarah was dancing with little Hans, telling him that soon they would be seeing his father again. Jenny wondered how Adam was, as she'd not seen him for some time. He was back in the house, she knew that, and after going once to see him there, she hadn't returned.

Their visit had ended acrimoniously. He had accused her of betrayal to her marriage vows and to him and had ended up calling her a slut, which was when Jenny had walked out of the house – and out of his life.

The next two months passed quickly, but for Jenny and Rusty it was a fraught time. If they were to go to America, there was so much to be done officially. Passports to be obtained, two copies of birth certificates, a statement from the husband or fiancé, and in some cases letters from the man's family. Evidence that they could afford a train ticket at the other end of their journey. For both the women, much that was needed was from the men, who were not around and as yet had not been in contact.

It was Brad who surfaced first of all. He managed to beg a space on a plane leaving Europe for London. There was no time to get in touch with Rusty, and as the aircraft landed in England, Brad decided just to make his way to Southampton. After all, Rusty would be at work, so calling her on the telephone would be difficult.

It was mid-afternoon, and Rusty had just finished serving a customer and was carefully folding one of the rejected garments, looking down at it, focusing on making it neat, when a hand caught hold of her wrist. She looked up in surprise and saw Brad! She felt the blood drain from her body, and her knees buckled.

Brad leapt the counter. 'It's all right, everybody, I'm a doctor!' he cried. 'Someone get me a glass of water.'

A few minutes later, Rusty started to come round and felt something cold against her forehead. She opened her eyes. 'Brad, Brad, was that really you?' she murmured.

'Yes, darling, it really is. How are you feeling?'

Rusty looked up at him and gave a wan smile.

'You could have given me a heart attack!'

He smoothed her cheek. 'For one awful moment, I thought I had.'

She looked around and saw lots of concerned faces staring down at her. 'Oh my God,' she whispered.

'It's all right, folks, the young lady is fine. She just fainted.' To the senior manager of the department, who had arrived to see what all the commotion was about, he said, 'I'm taking Miss Dobbs home. I doubt if she will be back for a few days.'

Once outside, Brad took her into his arms and kissed her longingly. 'I've waited for what seems a lifetime to do that,' he said. 'I'm taking you home. Let's find a taxi. Are you still at Chilworth?'

Rusty gave him her new address, saying, 'It's a long story, I'll explain later.'

Once they arrived at the flat in Hill Lane, Rusty made a cup of coffee and a sandwich for both of them and they sat on the settee and caught up with each other's news. Every now and again one would reach out to touch the other, as if trying to convince themselves that the other person was real.

Brad was sympathetic when he heard the news about Adam.

'That's a really tough deal,' he said. 'How did Jenny take it?'

Rusty tried to explain how difficult a decision it had been for her to keep her promise to Chad and put aside her feelings of guilt.

'Well, darling, life is cruel, I'm afraid. It throws

248

some diabolical curves your way, as if to say, now get out of that!' He pulled her towards him and looked into her eyes. 'I have to return to the States to be discharged, but I'm getting a special licence before I go, so we can be married.'

This took Rusty's breath away. 'Oh my God! Are you sure about this?'

'Absolutely! Why, have you any doubts?'

She threw her arms around his neck. 'Don't be ridiculous!' she cried – then she kissed him.

The next few days were frantic, trying to get ready for the wedding. Beth had offered to do the wedding breakfast as a present to the couple, and Jenny had one of her gowns altered for Rusty to wear. It was a coffee-coloured extravaganza bought before the war in an exclusive boutique in London. It was below the knee and fitted with a swathe across the neckline. It was very glamorous and expensive ... and looked it.

Rusty, with her auburn hair, beneath a small straw hat with a veil, was a perfect foil against the coffee shade of the dress. She carried a small bouquet of cream roses. Jenny was her maid of honour in a soft pale-green gown.

As the girls sat together in the wedding car, taking them to St Mark's church in Archers Road and a vicar who made time for them, they held hands.

Rusty was trembling. 'Is this really happening to me, Jenny?'

'Indeed it is, and for goodness sake, try and relax! This is a special day for any woman, so enjoy it. Now come on,' Jenny gently chided, 'there is nothing to be nervous about. Brad loves you, and you'll have a wonderful life.'

'Oh, I do know that, it just seems too good to be true. Until he puts that ring on my finger and we are declared man and wife, I won't believe it! I just wish you'd heard from Chad and that he could be here too.'

Jenny leaned out of the window of the vehicle. She had hoped by now to have had a letter from her lover. She wondered if he was still in Europe, waiting to be sent home, or was he already in the States? But why hadn't he written?

Brad had tried to trace his whereabouts for her, but had not been able to get a result with troops being moved hither and thither. 'Try not to fret, Jenny,' he told her. 'Chad will get back to you, of that I'm certain.'

The wedding was a quiet one, with only a few friends attending. Rusty didn't invite her mother, and her father was still in Australia, but it was a small but happy gathering of friends who were dear to her that sat at the table at Beth's house after the ceremony.

And after the speeches and the cake cutting, they all got changed out of their finery and went riding. It was a truly perfect ending to the day, with much merriment as they all rode through the woods together.

Later that night, in the honeymoon suite of the Polygon Hotel, Brad drew his bride into his arms. 'When we get home, we'll have a grand reception for the family.'

'That'll be nice,' Rusty said, 'except there won't

be anyone there to represent me.'

'We can invite Jenny and Chad,' he said, kissing her softly.

'What do you think has happened to him, Brad? I'm getting somewhat concerned for Jenny.'

'I've no idea, but I'm sure he's going to show up. He loves Jenny, he's not going to let her down.'

'But what if he believed Adam when he told Chad Jenny was staying with him?'

'Well, if I was in his shoes, Jenny would have to tell me to my face before I would believe it. Now, Mrs Jackson, your husband is waiting.' And he pulled her close.

Twenty-Seven

Little Hans had been fractious for a couple of days, and whatever Sarah tried to do seemed fruitless. The child wouldn't eat, he was restless and decidedly grumpy, and on the third day he started to cough and his temperature rose. He seemed to be having trouble with his breathing, and Sarah began to panic. She called to Beth to come and take a look at him.

Beth felt the baby's fevered forehead and noticed his laboured breathing. Calling for one of her staff to get the doctor, she took Sarah and the baby into the kitchen, where she boiled a kettle. When it was boiling, she made Sarah open an umbrella and hold it over her and Hans, making a canopy in which to hold the steam coming from the kettle. After a while, the child's breathing was easier, to everyone's relief, but the two women knew this was only a temporary measure. Hans was very poorly, and they were all relieved when, shortly after, the doctor arrived.

After examining the child, the doctor called an ambulance. 'Your baby is suffering with croup, and we need to get him to hospital and in a steam tent to relieve his breathing. This, hopefully, will help with the cough, and we need to get his temperature down. Has he eaten much?'

Sarah shook her head. 'He wouldn't take his milk or his cereal, nor would he drink the water in his bottle.'

The doctor frowned. 'He's probably dehydrated too.' Seeing the worried expression on Sarah's face, he lightly touched her arm. 'Try not to worry. In hospital they have all the equipment to get him better.'

But as she carried Hans into the ambulance, Sarah wasn't sure that that would be enough.

Beth had called Jenny's office the following morning to tell her about Hans and how poorly he was, so that evening she and Rusty went along to the hospital, armed with nightclothes for Sarah, who was sleeping in a chair next to the baby's cot; toiletries for her use; grapes and sandwiches to eat; and magazines to read.

Sarah looked distraught, and when she saw the two women she burst into tears.

Whilst Jenny was comforting the girl, Rusty poured a cup of strong tea from a flask and slipped two lumps of sugar in. She stirred this and handed it to Sarah. 'Here, drink this, love, it'll make you feel better.'

Whilst Sarah was resting, drinking her tea and having a snack – to build her strength, as she was told – the two friends were looking at Hans in his steam tent.

'Ah, bless him,' said Rusty. 'Will you just look at the little chap? He does look so pale, but this contraption seems to be working, as his breathing isn't too laboured.'

'He still has that hacking croupy cough,' Sarah told them. 'It sounds so awful, almost as if it's coming from his little boots.' She fished in her pocket and held out a crumpled sheet of paper. 'If I give you the address, will you send this to Gunter for me? I need him to know about Hans. He is his father, and he has the right to know.'

Jenny took it from her. 'I'll catch the last post tonight,' she promised.

Gunter eagerly opened the letter the following afternoon, anxious to see what Sarah had to say. These letters were like a lifeline to him and kept him going during his imprisonment, but when he read the content he went pale. He quickly read it again, before heading for the office where the English captain, who was in charge of camp, was to be found. He asked permission to see him on compassionate grounds.

Once inside the office, he stood to attention.

'Well, Reinhardt, what is it that brings you here to see me?'

Gunter handed the officer the letter he'd just received.

The captain read the contents, frowned, handed back the letter and said, 'I'm sorry to hear about your son. I hope he gets better soon.'

'I would like your permission to go and see him, sir. I realize this is asking a lot, but he's only a few months old, and I've only seen him when he was very small. I've missed so much of him growing, and now he's really sick; you can imagine my concern.'

'Yes, of course I do. I have children myself. But I'm afraid that's not possible.' As Gunter started to protest, the officer interrupted him. 'I will, however, allow you to make one call to the hospital to find out for yourself exactly what the situation is – but Reinhardt, that is all I can do.'

'Very well, sir, thank you.'

Gunter was led into the outer office, where the clerk found the hospital number, dialled it, then handed the receiver over.

He was eventually put through to the ward where Hans was being cared for. 'My name is Gunter Reinhardt. I wish to know how my small son, Hans, is doing. He was brought in yesterday.'

'One moment, Mr Reinhardt, I'll get Matron.'

Gunter listened to the woman as she told him of Hans' condition. Gunter looked even more concerned as he listened, until the matron said, 'Would you like a word with your wife? She's here with the baby.'

'Thank you, I would appreciate that.'

'Hello?' There was a tentative note in Sarah's voice.

'Sarah, *liebling,* it's me, Gunter!'

'Gunter! When they said my husband was on the phone, I wondered who on earth it was. Oh Gunter, if only you were here. Hans is so poorly. They have him in a steam tent for his breathing, but his cough sounds awful!' She started to cry, which tore him apart.

He tried to comfort her, but felt absolutely hopeless. 'I am so sorry that you have to face this alone. I've asked to see Hans, but they won't let me, I was only allowed this call. Oh Sarah, try not to worry.'

Between sobs she told him that Jenny, Beth and Rusty were keeping her company. 'But the only person I want with me is you!'

Gunter was so frustrated. He desperately wanted to be there with Sarah and his son, and he wondered just how he'd get through the next few days, which the matron had said were crucial for the little baby.

'I have to go, Gunter, Hans is crying. I'll write to you every day. I love you.'

He didn't even have time to say goodbye. He handed back the receiver to the soldier on duty and walked back to his room, but he just couldn't settle. Eventually, he walked outside and wandered around. He had to get out of the camp somehow and see his boy.

Parked outside the camp kitchen was a lorry delivering vegetables to the cook. The driver picked up a large sack of potatoes and carried it into the kitchen. The German saw the name of the company on the side of the van, and when he saw it gave an address in Southampton, he made a quick decision. He swiftly climbed into the back of the lorry, saw an old mac on the floor and picked it up before burying himself beneath a pile of empty sacks. He heard the driver return, and he held his breath. To his relief, the man closed the back doors to the van and, climbing into the driver's seat, drove out of the camp.

Gunter had no idea where he was headed and how he would find his way to the hospital, but at least he was out of the camp, and somehow he *would* see his sick boy. He had the address of the hospital in the letter Sarah had sent.

The journey seemed to take a long time, and Gunter wondered when the vehicle would stop. Eventually, it did so, and he heard the driver get out and walk away. He carefully got to his feet and peered through the small windows of the door. They seemed to have stopped outside a warehouse, and he saw a man he presumed to be the driver walk into the vast interior.

Gunter quickly opened the doors of the van, closed them behind him and slipped inside the building. Fortunately, everyone inside seemed to be too busy to notice him, and when he saw a man emerge from a nearby room, he noticed through the open door a row of coats hanging. He waited, then walked over to the door casually and, with baited breath, opened it. Luckily for him, there was no one inside.

He quickly looked for a coat that would fit him. He tried one on and felt in the pocket, where to his delight he found some loose change. He swiftly went through the pockets of the others and soon had a small collection of coins. Opening the door of the cloakroom, he looked out and, seeing that no one seemed to be nearby, he slipped out and walked purposefully out of the building.

Once clear, he looked around for someone to ask about the hospital he wanted to visit. He approached an elderly lady and politely asked her. To his great relief he was in Southampton, as he hoped.

The unsuspecting woman gave him detailed instructions, even to which tram to catch – which would take him almost to the door. He thanked her and made his way to the tram stop.

Sarah was sitting by Hans – who, in his steam tent, was sleeping peacefully – turning the pages of a magazine. She looked up as she heard footsteps approaching. She frowned. That man walking down the ward looked just like Gunter, she thought, but how ridiculous! He was in civilian clothes, and Gunter was in Bishop's Waltham. But there was something about him that made her keep watching. She was about to cry out as he got nearer, but the man put his finger to his lips, so she covered her mouth to smother the sound which was rising in her throat.

When he reached her, he kissed her quickly and whispered, 'Don't say anything, *liebling,* I'm here. Let's make the most of the time we have together. Now let me see my son.'

Sarah could hardly believe what was happening, and after she'd told him the latest news of little Hans, and held on to Gunter's arm to make sure he was real, she couldn't wait any longer.

'Gunter, what on earth are you doing here? I thought you were unable to come.'

He held her to him. 'I escaped from the camp, and soon they'll discover I'm missing. They'll probably find me pretty soon, knowing my son is sick, so we may not have much time.' He gazed into her eyes and kissed her passionately. 'I had to come. How could I let you face this without me?'

'You'll be in so much trouble!' she exclaimed.

'What can they do to me, Sarah? I am already a prisoner. But I had to see Hans and you.'

'The doctor says that probably tomorrow Hans can come out of the tent, as his breathing is so much better.'

'That's marvellous news,' he said, reaching in the tent to hold his baby's hand. He smiled as he looked at his son. 'He has grown so much, it's amazing.'

Gunter was still there in the late afternoon when Rusty and Jenny called into the ward. Sarah introduced them, saying, 'He won't be here long, as they will have discovered he's missing at roll call this evening.'

Jenny looked at the happy expression on Sarah's face, but she knew that the situation wasn't good. 'May I make a suggestion?'

They looked at her with puzzled expressions.

'It would be better for Gunter if he went back to the camp under his own steam. The consequences would not be so severe. I'd be happy to drive him back there. What do you think? After all, these are compassionate grounds. If he goes back without waiting for them to come and get him, they may look upon the whole thing more kindly.'

Gunter looked at Sarah and smiled. 'Your friend makes sense, *liebling*. Now I've seen you and Hans, I can sleep at night without worry.'

She hugged him. 'Go, darling, I don't want you to get into too much trouble. It was wonderful to see you, but you need to leave now before it's too late.'

And so Jenny and Rusty bundled the young man into the back of the car and drove out to Bishop's Waltham.

Jenny stopped just short of the camp and let the German out. 'Please don't worry about your family,' she told him. 'Whilst Rusty and I are about, we'll make sure she and the baby are fine.'

'Thank you so much, I don't know what to say. Sarah is so lucky to have such good friends.'

'You had better go,' said Jenny. 'With a bit of luck no one has yet left to search for you, which will only help your cause.'

The two women watched him walk up to the gate and be stopped by the guard. As they let him through, Gunter turned and smiled.

'Nice chap,' said Jenny as she drove away. 'I'm so pleased we met him, because now we know that Sarah has a good man.'

'Nothing's easy though, is it?' said Rusty wryly. 'There he is, supposedly the enemy, now with an English wife and baby. Her parents have disowned her, and who knows how his family will react to his situation once he's repatriated?'

'From what I saw today, if his parents didn't approve, I don't think it would make any difference to Gunter. Did you see the way he looked at Sarah? And he's naturally crazy about his son. No, nothing will keep them apart but time!'

Apart from a serious reprimand, Gunter Reinhardt was spared further punishment. The fact he returned voluntarily, and before the military police had been sent to find him, stood him in good stead. He was able to write to Sarah and tell her the good news. A few days after, she was able to write and tell him that little Hans was being allowed home, which was a great relief to all.

Twenty-Eight

Chad Maxwell had been in a military hospital in Southern France, suffering with a severe bout of bronchitis, which had laid him low. He'd been too ill to enjoy the celebrations when the end of the war was declared; all he knew was that he had to get better. But before he was fully recovered, he was shipped home, spending the voyage in the ship's hospital.

When the liner docked in New York, he made the journey home to Wyoming, staying with his parents until he was better. There he told them about the wonderful girl he was going to marry.

'So when do we get to meet this Jenny?' asked his father.

'When I have a home to offer her, Dad. I need to buy a ranch so we can raise horses. She's given up so much for me, I want her to be happy.'

'She needs a ranch to make her happy?' asked the elder Maxwell.

'Hell no! She said she would sleep on a blanket in the open as long as she's with me.'

'Then why the devil are you wasting your time? Bring her out here!'

'It's not that simple, Dad. She's married and has to get a divorce, and there is a great deal of paperwork to get done before we can be together.'

'She knows you're home, son?'

'I've not had the opportunity to write. First I was ill, then I was on a ship, now the journey here.'

'You're taking a chance, aren't you, my boy? How do you know she's still waiting for you?'

'I don't, Dad, and to be honest it scares the hell out of me.' He then explained to his father the predicament he discovered when he saw Adam.

His father frowned. 'Well, Chad, do you believe the man?'

'To be honest, I don't know. I realize that Jenny would feel she had a duty to stay with him, under the circumstances, but I also know how we felt about each other. I want her with me, but I feel a louse to even think of her leaving a man who has lost his sight!'

'Then you must go back there and sort this out! Once you've been discharged, you must go back to England. You can't get on with your life, Chad, until you do. You know that, don't you?'

'You're right, of course. But first I have to get my discharge. Then I'll sort it, I promise.'

Back in Southampton, Jenny carried on working, sorting out the paperwork and getting the GI brides ready for the voyage that would send them off to a new country and a new life, all the time wishing it were her that was going.

She and Brad had pulled a few strings to enable Rusty to stay in the flat, instead of joining the other brides at Tidworth camp, whilst awaiting passage to America. He had now left the country and was home, discharged from the army and setting up his practice once again.

Rusty was kept informed of his every move by letters which came regularly, which only made it more difficult for Jenny, who had heard nothing from Chad. Jenny had also been served divorce papers by Adam's solicitor and was visiting her own solicitor to enable the case to go to court, but it was a long and arduous task. As she wasn't disputing the charge of adultery, she wouldn't have to appear in court, for which she was eternally grateful.

Meantime, Chad was having a hard time booking a cabin on one of the *Queens* to travel from New York to Southampton. The bookings were full, and he was on a waiting list. He'd written to Jenny, telling her of his plans ... but this letter wasn't readdressed to her, because the time had run out at the post office, and it landed in Adam's hands, who put it in the dustbin, unopened.

It was now September, and Jenny had still had no word from the horse whisperer, but she tried not to be too disheartened. She couldn't help the doubts which kept creeping into her mind that once Chad had arrived home things had changed, but deep down she really believed she'd see him again. There had been a sincerity about the American that was unshakeable in her mind, and on the darkest days she clung to this hope.

She spent her spare time at the stables with Beth. For Jenny it was cathartic, cleaning out the stables, rubbing the horses down and taking them out on exercise, letting them gallop, feeling the wind through her hair – being alone with her thoughts.

Today she'd been out with one of the stallions for a good hour, giving him a thorough workout and then a run, and she rode back into the stables in good spirits, having benefited as much as the animal. She slipped out of the saddle, watered the horse, then led him into his stable where she removed the saddle and the rest of the tack, wiping him down after she'd done so. All the time talking softly to the horse, engrossed in what she was doing.

'I do believe I could train you to do my job.'

Jenny froze. She could hardly believe her ears. Turning, she saw Chad leaning over the stable door, grinning broadly at her.

'Hello, Jenny honey. Sorry it took me so long to get here, but here I am.'

With a loud cry of delight, Jenny ran to the door which Chad had now opened, to be lifted off her feet as she flew into his arms.

'I knew you'd come!' she cried as she rained kisses on him.

Beth and the others came running at the sounds of excitement, and Chad was made welcome by them all.

'Hey, it's great to be back and see you guys again,' he said, all the time keeping his arm around Jenny.

She looked at Chad and frowned.

'What's the matter, honey?' he asked.

'I'm trying to think what's different, but of course, you're not in uniform, that's what's different!'

Chad was wearing a pair of dark-brown trousers and a tan leather coat. He looked very smart, but it did seem strange to see him out of uniform.

Beth sent them into the house so they could be together and alone. 'But you can make us all a cup of tea in half an hour,' she told him as she walked away, laughing.

Once in the kitchen, Chad took Jenny into his arms. 'Here, let me look at you,' he said as he caressed her face. 'God! How I've missed you. I was almost afraid to come here this morning in case you sent me away.'

'Did you believe what Adam said, then?' asked Jenny.

'I didn't want to, but you know, the poor guy was blind. That's why I sent the flowers, to let you know I still felt the same.'

'What flowers?'

'After I saw Adam, I went to the florist and sent flowers with a message.'

Jenny shook her head. 'I never did see them. Adam must have got rid of them.'

Pulling her close to him, Chad said quietly,

264

'You couldn't blame him, honey. He was fighting to keep you. I'd have probably done the same.' He gazed fondly at her. 'My folks are very anxious to meet you.'

'Do they know I'm married, waiting on a divorce?'

'Yes, they know. They also know that I love you and we are going to be together.'

'How long are you here for?' Jenny asked.

'As long as it takes to get the situation sorted. I'm not leaving here until you can come with me.'

'My divorce comes up next week. Then I'll have to wait six weeks before it's finalized and I get my decree nisi. I don't have to go, as I'm not contesting it. I'm afraid he named you, Chad, as the man I was consorting with.'

He grinned broadly. 'Consorting, eh? Well, I guess that's one way of putting it. What say we make Beth her tea and then go back to your place and consort?'

Jenny started to laugh. 'It makes sex sound kind of legal, doesn't it?'

He kissed her soundly. 'I don't care how it sounds, honey. Let's just go and do it before I lose my mind waiting. It's been a long time.'

After the divorce, Jenny and Chad waited for six weeks for the decree nisi and then they were married by special licence at the registry office in Southampton. Rusty and Beth were witnesses as the two of them took their vows. After which the four of them went to the Dolphin Hotel for a champagne lunch.

Chad reached for Jenny's hand. 'Sorry this wasn't perhaps the wedding you dreamed of, darlin', but when we get home we'll have a church blessing with the family and friends.'

'It really isn't important, Chad.' She held out her hand and gazed at her shiny new wedding ring. 'What's important is that we are married. The rest is all just stuff!'

'I love this woman!' he joked. 'I'll never have to spend a fortune on her, she said she'd live with me on a blanket outside if need be. Well, Jenny honey, I took you at your word. At home I bought us a couple of Indian blankets! Who needs a home – it's just stuff!'

Gunter Reinhardt had returned to Germany with the other prisoners and like the Americans had been discharged from the army. To his delight, when he returned to his hometown, he found his home intact and the office where he was training was still in business. His parents were alive; his father had survived the fighting, and his mother had escaped the worst of the raids by staying with relatives.

They were somewhat shocked to discover that he had fathered a son with an English girl, but when he showed them the pictures of young Hans and Sarah that she'd sent to him, they were intrigued by their grandson.

As soon as he was able, Gunter arrived back in Southampton to take Sarah to Germany to be married. She introduced him to Beth and all the staff at the stables, and then they travelled by bus to visit the Browns.

Ethel Brown was delighted to see them and made a great fuss of Hans. She insisted they stay, and when Gunter queried the wisdom of this, she said, 'The war is over! The sooner we get over it the better!'

At lunchtime when the farmer returned with his son, Sarah and Gunter were a bit apprehensive, but the young man surprised them. He shook Gunter by the hand. 'My dad is always telling me how hard you worked whilst you were here and that he couldn't have managed without you, so thanks for that. No hard feelings?'

'No, indeed. Your parents were wonderful to me and to Sarah. I will always be in their debt.'

'That's enough of that,' Arthur Brown said. 'Let's eat. I'm starving!'

The following week, Gunter took Sarah and their son across the channel by ferry and on the train to his home and family, where they were greeted warmly. Fortunately for her, his parents spoke English, but as his mother said, 'Once you get settled in and married, you will have to shop, so you'll need to learn the language.' At the look of trepidation on Sarah's face, she smiled. 'Don't worry, being in the country will help you to pick it up, but you must speak English to little Hans, then he'll grow up knowing both languages automatically. I'll help you.'

And she did. By the time Gunter had found a house for them and arranged a wedding, Sarah was already making progress with the language and finding that Gunter's family accepted her without difficulty. For once, she felt part of a real family, and she blossomed.

It was January that they were married in a little local church with his family and friends assembled. Farmer Brown and his wife had travelled there, with Beth to give Sarah some support. Rusty and Jenny would have gone too, but Rusty was booked on a ship to take her to New York, and Chad was trying to get himself and Jenny a berth on the *Aquitania,* but they sent gifts and a telegram of good wishes.

Sarah sent her father a picture of her wedding and of Hans, but she ignored her mother. As far as Sarah was concerned, she didn't have one.

The day arrived when Rusty left Southampton and, with the hundreds of other GI brides, sailed out of the port for New York and a new life. For some, when they reached their destination, it would be like being in heaven; sadly, for others it would be like hell on earth. But as the ship left the harbour, every one of them had a head full of dreams.

Beth, Chad and Jenny waved to Rusty from the quayside. Brad was meeting her in New York, and he'd invited Chad and Jenny to visit at any time. Rusty made her promise she'd keep in touch and that when they were both in the States they would visit each other at least once a year. She had given her word.

It took some further three weeks until Chad and Jenny were due to leave England for Wyoming. They had been to the American Embassy in London, filled in all the necessary papers, taken the medical and satisfied the authorities that financially they were secure. Chad's father stood as guarantee for Jenny over and above his son, her husband. The American Embassy demanded a lot before they gave Mrs Chad Maxwell her visa.

Beth gave them a small farewell dinner, which was attended by the staff and a few friends. It was a happy occasion, and as they walked around the stables after, they talked about their first meeting and how their lives had changed.

'It's the crazy war, Jenny honey. Everything changes in one way or another. Some changes are for the good, and others, not so. It brought me you, so I was the lucky one. And believe me I'm going to make sure I deserved the break. We are going to have a great life together. You will learn to love my country as I learned to love yours, and we'll come back now and again to see it.'

'Can we do that, really?'

'Sure we can. This is where your roots are and will always be. No one can take that away from you ever, nor should they want to.'

She put her arms around his neck. 'Mr Maxwell, you have a great understanding of what goes on in the mind.'

'Of course I do, Jenny honey, I'm a horse whisperer, it's part of the job!'

'I just can't wait to use those Indian blankets you bought,' she teased.

'I can't wait to see you among my friends with your quaint English ways. Wait until you introduce them to teatime!'

Laughing she said, 'With cucumber sandwiches, scones and crumpets.'

'What the hell are crumpets? It sounds like an illness.'

She laughed loudly. 'You have a lot to learn, cowboy!'

He chuckled. 'You think so? Wait until you come on a round-up and have to cook on a chuck wagon!' He drew her to him and kissed her. 'We are going to have so much fun, you and I. And when we are old and grey, we'll sit on our porch in the twilight and reminisce of how we met and the trials and tribulations we went through to be together.'

She smiled softly. She would always think affectionately of Chad as her guilty pleasure, which sounded a little naughty to her still, although they were now married. She hoped that one day Adam would find a little of the happiness she felt; then it would be a really fitting end to everything. She was now Mrs Chad Maxwell, and that was enough for her.

The publishers hope that this book has given you enjoyable reading. Large Print Books are especially designed to be as easy to see and hold as possible. If you wish a complete list of our books please ask at your local library or write directly to:

Magna Large Print Books
Magna House, Long Preston,
Skipton, North Yorkshire.
BD23 4ND

This Large Print Book for the partially sighted, who cannot read normal print, is published under the auspices of

THE ULVERSCROFT FOUNDATION